GOODWILL FOR THE GENTLEMAN

Belles of Christmas Book Two

MARTHA KEYES

D0326062

"I thought you said it was a private gathering," he said to Captain Gillingham, a touch of annoyance in his voice.

"And so it is," Gillingham responded cheerfully through his turtle mask, admiring the woman passing by in a shimmering gown meant to resemble fish scales. "Hardly a soul here! Everyone's left town already for the holidays."

Hugh scoffed. "You could have fooled me. It bears a strong resemblance to the last masquerade I attended at Vauxhall Gardens three years ago—and that was hardly exclusive."

"Bah! Vauxhall would have ten times this many people. I'll tell you what—you've become too accustomed to solitude." Gillingham clapped Hugh on the back of his black domino. "Come, Warrilow."

Hugh grabbed his friend's arm. "Don't use my name, for heaven's sake," he said through a tight jaw, glancing around to see if anyone was listening.

Gillingham shot him a troubled look. "If you're heading for home, Warrilow, it's only a matter of time before it's out that you've returned."

"Yes," said Hugh, "but I would much rather that the news come out when I am *not* here to witness its effect."

Gillingham clucked his tongue. "This won't do at all! Let down your hair. Live a little. It's high time you enjoyed yourself for a change. One doesn't take a leave of absence to go hide in a cave, man!"

"If one has my reputation, one just might," Hugh said dryly.

It was foolish to have let Gillingham persuade him into coming. The only thing standing between him and appalled glances was his mask. He *should* have made his way home from Spain directly to the family estate at Norfield—as he had planned to do—rather than agreeing to break his journey in London for a few days. Or he might have even gone to Grindleham, the Warrilows' small estate in Derbyshire, for a chance to adjust to life in England before seeing his family. And yet, here he was.

Gillingham had always had a way of cajoling Hugh into agreeing to his plans.

"Your reputation?" Gillingham spat out. "That was years ago. You know as well as I that society has a memory for scandal shorter than Prinny's breath."

Hugh wished he could believe that. He wished his *own* memory was as fickle as Gillingham seemed to think the *ton's* memory was. But surely one never forgot the looks and whispers which had followed Hugh so doggedly, until he had decided to accept his uncle's offer to buy a commission. In many ways, the battlefield had been a welcome reprieve.

He rubbed at his shoulder and winced. Of course, not all of it had been a reprieve. Not by any stretch of the imagination.

Gillingham shook his head, his eyes wide with wonder behind his black domino as he admired the scene. "I had forgotten how much I missed England. No offense to *las señoritas españolas*, of course," he added quickly, "but I am tolerably certain that nothing can compare to an accomplished English lady."

Hugh was silent, but he found himself in agreement with his friend. He had been close enough to swearing off his home country forever, to staying in Spain where he had a fresh start, a clean slate. But there was something extraordinary about England and her people.

Hugh was glad to be back.

Of course, for all his family knew, he was still in Spain. Just as likely, they thought him dead.

It had been months and months since he had written to them, after all.

He worried his lip, thinking about the reception he was likely to receive from them. Whatever their reactions might be, he could hardly blame them after he had neglected to inform them of his injury and his intent to return.

He had his reasons, though. At first, the ball in his shoulder had prevented it. Then it was the subsequent illness and the all-encompassing grief at losing Robert Seymour.

He shook his head. He didn't want to think on that right now. There would be more than enough time for it once he was back at Norfield.

Regardless, holding a quill to paper had been the last thing on his mind after his injury. And then it had been easy to continue putting it off for one reason or another. Before he knew it, he had begun to wonder if perhaps his family wasn't better off without him—better off believing him dead or disappeared like the coward so many believed him to be.

But in the end, he realized he couldn't stay away from England, from his mother—from his past. Everyone else might come to forget him in his absence, forget the shame he bore, but he wouldn't have forgotten, no matter how long he stayed away.

Gillingham grabbed his arm with an intake of breath. "Come. I must dance with that young woman over there." He indicated a young lady wearing a gold domino and cat ears, standing—quite strangely—alone.

"Do you know her?"

"No," Gillingham reasoned, "but how is *she* to know that? After all, a masquerade is the only ball where I can conceivably approach a stranger and ask her to dance." He grinned, and Hugh shook his head with a chuckle, following alongside him.

He would accompany Gillingham without complaint, but it was a waste of time for Hugh to set his own sights on any of the women in attendance. At least he assumed so. Who would wish to dance with a man reputed to be a jilt? Of course, his mask kept them from *knowing* such a thing, but it felt wrong to take advantage of their ignorance.

"My lady," Gillingham said in his most alluring voice as they came upon the young woman.

She turned, and Hugh noted her almond-shaped eyes of blue-flecked gray, which peered at him through her cat mask. He felt his heart rate pick up slightly and shook away the thought of two women he knew with just such pairs of eyes.

"Might I persuade you," Gillingham continued, "to stand up with me for the next set?" He extended a hand toward her, dipping into an overly-formal bow.

A woman in a tiger mask and an orange- and black-striped, hooded domino approached them, coming shoulder-to-shoulder with the woman in the cat mask as she glanced at Gillingham's extended hand.

"Lucy," she said, shooting a watchful glance at Hugh and Gillingham. "I thought you were with Mr. Pritchard or I shouldn't have left you."

Hugh stilled, glancing back and forth between the two women, his wide eyes lingering on the hooded one: her confident posture, her direct gaze, the color of her caramel brown hair that peeked out from her hood. He would recognize her anywhere, domino or no.

It was Emma Caldwell, the woman he had loved—the woman he hoped fervently that he didn't *still* love—and beside her Lucy Caldwell, the woman he had jilted.

Hugh's jaw clenched, and he suppressed the impulse to check that his mask was still on. He wasn't ready to face the Caldwells. Not just yet.

His first act upon arrival in England had been to inquire as subtly as possible whether the Caldwell sisters were—as he assumed they would be—married. He had hoped that Emma, at least, would have married, for it would have been a type of forced closure to his abominably persistent affection.

But neither had married during his absence. This was perhaps not a surprise for Emma, as she had often proclaimed her lack of desire to marry. But Lucy...he trusted that she had reasons beyond any related to Hugh and his purposeful rejection of her.

Either way, he had to do what he came to do: repair the brokenness he'd left behind him when he'd gone off to war. He had to face up to it, and that meant making things right with Lucy—it meant offering now what he hadn't been able to bring himself to offer three years ago: marriage.

At the time, he had rationalized his choice—they hadn't been formally engaged, after all. But the arrangement between the families had been long-standing: that Hugh, the heir of Norfield would marry Lucy, the eldest of the Caldwells. It had made perfect sense to his own parents and to Lucy's parents.

But it had made no sense to Hugh's heart, which had stubbornly latched onto Emma and dug in its heels at any of Hugh's attempts to change its affections. His heart simply refused to give up the confident, bold protector he had seen Emma become. How ironic that it was what he loved so well about Emma that had ensured she would never forgive him.

But, hated by Emma or no, he had simply not been able to subject Lucy to marrying a man who was in love with her sister.

He'd had three years away from Emma, though—long enough, he hoped, for his heart to see sense; or at least to subject itself to his strengthened determination. He knew now that there were more important things in life than following his heart: he had a duty to his family and to Norfield. Lucy might reject his offer of marriage, and she might well hate him, but Hugh was prepared to face that if it meant a chance of righting the wrong he had done years ago—a chance to prove himself.

At least Lucy would no longer be laboring under the misapprehension that he was some sort of *nonpareil,* as she had thought him to be before it had all happened.

A man strode up, his fiery red hair set off by the blue of his domino, his face masked in black. He bowed slightly to Hugh and Gillingham before offering an arm to the young woman in gold—to Lucy.

"Ah, my apologies," Gillingham said, clearing his throat. "I see that I am too late in my request." He smiled at the man in the blue domino without any rancor. "But don't let that prevent the two of you —" he indicated Hugh and Emma — "from joining the set."

Hugh clenched his teeth, wanting nothing more than to strangle his friend. But that was not an option, and for the first time in three years, Emma's eyes looked at him.

He had been haunted by those gray eyes since his sudden departure; haunted by the cold contempt they had held when she had last looked on him. Any flicker of hope he had been harboring that she would forgive him for jilting Lucy had disappeared in that moment.

His first inclination was to make his excuses to Emma, to avoid the prospect of standing up together for a set. If they danced, she was bound to discover his identity, and what would she do then? She was quite capable of deserting him on the dance floor. He could almost see the look of revulsion that would transform her otherwise-kind eyes.

He shuddered slightly. The prospect was too reminiscent of their last encounter. It brought flashbacks of the humiliation that had consumed him and the astounded faces that had surrounded him when she had given him the cut direct in just such a ballroom as this.

A fourth gentleman joined the group, coming up beside Emma. Hugh swallowed the lump in his throat. Who was the gentleman? According to a mutual acquaintance, she wasn't married. But was she engaged? His heart dropped.

"I am afraid I must ask your pardon," Emma said. "I am promised to stand up with Mr. Douglas." She indicated the man beside her.

Hugh bowed politely, feeling relief as well as regret, then put a firm hand on Gillingham's shoulders and pulled him away.

"Confound it," Gillingham said. "Should have known the angel would be spoken for with a smile like that. I should have asked her to save me the next set, but with that fellow's eyes boring into me, I lost my nerve."

Hugh was silent, feeling the beads of sweat which were gathering at his hairline. How had he not considered that he might happen upon the Misses Caldwell at the masquerade? He had assumed that they would already be at home for Christmas. The Caldwells took the holiday season very seriously.

It hadn't taken him more than two minutes in Emma's presence, though, to feel the magnetic draw to her; the pull that he fervently hoped had dissipated during his time on the Continent.

But perhaps it was simply the unexpectedness of the encounter in combination with his nerves that he had mistaken for lingering romantic attraction?

He sincerely hoped so.

THE VIOLINS STRUNG out the last notes of a cotillion, and Emma's partner, Mr. Douglas, bowed. She took the opportunity to steal a curious glance at the man her sister Lucy was promised to marry, who was making his bow next to Mr. Douglas.

Mr. George Pritchard was nothing like the sort of man she had expected Lucy to wed, with his close-cropped red hair, freckles, and bland gaze.

He must have felt Emma's eyes on him, since he looked over at her as he straightened. He offered an abashed smile before turning his head away, as if embarrassed he had caught her looking at him.

She kept her eyes on him, one side of her mouth tilting upward at his behavior. At least he was kind. Perhaps that was all that mattered.

"It was an honor to stand up with you, Miss Caldwell," said Mr. Douglas, taking a step toward her.

She smiled politely. A dance with Mr. Douglas was very much like any other dance—full of civil small-talk and polite smiles. But that was what Emma needed: someone ordinary and reliable; someone she could respect but never fall in love with; someone with the ability to make her comfortable but without the ability to hurt her.

"I understand," Mr. Douglas continued, "that you are to journey home for the holidays."

She nodded. "Yes, my mother is staunchly traditional, you know, and she insists that we all return home to celebrate the season together. It is her idea of heaven, and she guards it somewhat aggressively."

Mr. Douglas nodded his understanding. "She is German, is she not?"

"Yes, and very proud of it, too," Emma said with a significant look. "At this time of year more than any other."

"I should very much like to meet her. Allow me to wish you a very happy Christmas with your family. I hope that, once your father has returned to town, I might perhaps beg an audience with him." His brows raised in a question.

Emma felt her stomach clench oddly. Ignoring a silly reaction to a very expected comment, she nodded with a smile and bid him goodbye.

It was precisely what she had been planning for, so there was no reason to regard a bit of unease. Surely it was natural to feel nervous at the prospect of marriage, something she had been putting off for so long.

She turned to Lucy, who was watching Mr. Pritchard walk off, his blue domino sweeping behind him.

"He is very amiable, Lucy. I think you have done well." Emma tilted her head as she watched him. "Though he is perhaps not precisely the type of gentleman I had pictured you marrying."

Lucy turned toward her, drawing her head back slightly with a frown. "What kind of gentleman *did* you think I should marry?" Her voice was soft, just like her kind eyes and the ringlets which hung loosely on her shoulders.

Emma narrowed her eyes in thought. "I think I assumed that you would marry someone a bit taller. More imposing and protective. And though I am beginning to think it very distinguished, the red hair was certainly unexpected." She sent Lucy a teasing smile.

"Oh?" Lucy said, amused. "I had no idea you had such an opinion on the matter. Anything else, pray?"

Emma nodded with a teasing smile. It was absurd of her to have acquired such strong beliefs about the appearance and character of Lucy's future husband. And yet she *had* acquired them. "Perhaps just one or two more things: formidable on first inspection, but with a soft light in his eyes and a kind heart."

Emma was only half teasing. Lucy needed someone to guard the quiet, sensitive woman she was—to protect her from any more pain. She needed a gentle gentleman. Mr. Pritchard was both gentle and a gentleman, of course. He simply looked too slight to act as much of a protector.

"This is all very enlightening. And what if *I* should take it upon myself to find a husband for you?" Lucy suggested.

Emma let out a small laugh, and she wrapped her arm into Lucy's. "I think you would do a fine job of choosing a husband for me —if only I hadn't already decided upon one myself."

Lucy ignored her words, scanning the crowd until her eyes stopped. "Hmm...what of Lord Whitfield?"

Emma followed her sister's gaze to the earl. He wore no costume, providing quite a contrast to his friend beside him, dressed in a very extravagant lion costume.

Emma looked at Lucy with incredulous brows. "Perhaps we shouldn't aim quite so high, Lucy."

Lucy sighed. "Very well." She continued scanning the room. "Ah, and what about the man in the black, eagle mask from earlier? The one you were to dance with? There was something a bit mysterious about him, I think, and *everyone* likes mystery."

Emma laughed. "Mysterious? Perhaps because he didn't say a single word? *Or* because he is wearing an enormous bird mask. The entire purpose of a masquerade is to give us the illusion of mystery, isn't it?"

"There would be less mystery if you danced with him." Lucy wagged her brows once. "Or married him, even," she said with a playful shrug.

Emma clucked her tongue. "As I said, it is a terrible shame that I have already settled upon who I am to marry."

Lucy sighed, giving up the game. "Mr. Douglas?"

Emma nodded with a laugh. "Why should you say it in such a voice? He is perfectly respectable."

"Never mind," Lucy said resignedly. "Are you sure you don't

wish to travel with us to Barthorpe Hall? We leave tomorrow morning, and George insists it would be no trouble at all to have you stay there with us for two or three days. We will be to Marsdon by the 23rd at the very latest, in plenty of time to help Mama decorate."

Emma smiled but shook her head. "It is very kind of him, but I still have a number of things to do before leaving town." She shifted her jaw, thinking of the letter she had received. "Besides, I've just received a letter from Papa. He has asked that I break my journey for dinner at Norfield to convey his congratulations and a gift to Alfred and his new fiancée." She shot Lucy a significant look. "I doubt that is something you would like to do—particularly in the company of George." If George Pritchard knew of Lucy's past with Hugh Warrilow, it would likely be uncomfortable for him.

Lucy's own eyebrows shot up. "Surely between you and me, there is little doubt who relishes the thought of a visit to Norfield Manor less. You can't even bring yourself to *say* Hugh Warrilow's name—how will you fare, dining at his home where he is very likely to come up in conversation? Where there will be reminders of him everywhere?"

Emma said nothing for a moment. His was a name that made her blood boil, even three years later.

Lucy sought her eyes. "You prove my point with your silence." She sighed and shook her head. "How you can go from cheering on a match between Hugh and myself, touting his best qualities, to despising him so—it isn't reasonable, Emma."

Emma *had* thought Hugh a wonderful match for Lucy at one time. In fact, Emma's description—*imposing but kind and gentle*—was an apt description of the man Emma had once thought Hugh was —the perfect man to protect Lucy's pure and guileless heart.

But instead of shielding Lucy as he should have, he had left her vulnerable, subjected her to scorn and heartache.

Emma clenched one of her gloved hands. The memory of Lucy's anguish—her lovely, kind eyes set within two dark hollows, the way they filled up with tears at the least provocation—it still felt fresh to

Emma. Lucy would be a married woman soon and seemed to have moved past what had happened, but Emma could never forget how Lucy's broken heart had seemed to break her spirit for so long.

Emma took a glass of negus from the silver tray held by a passing footman and handed it to Lucy before taking one for herself. "I am very fond of Lady Dayton, and I have no need to fret over being confronted by Hugh Warrilow—"

"I believe he is a lieutenant now," Lucy said.

Emma tilted her head. "I am sure you are right. But who is to say, when he has made no effort to write his family? He could be anywhere, in any state, really." She shrugged lightly. "I think it likely that he has met the same sad fate as so many other soldiers have."

Lucy lowered her glass. "If that is so, it is not something to take pleasure in, Emma. It is terribly sad. Lady Dayton only recently told me that she feels she must accept that he is dead. And I fear she may be right. Mrs. Seymour's husband was fighting in Spain, too, you know, and *she* received the tragic news of his death months ago. That Lord and Lady Dayton have had not a word from Hugh for so long does not bode well."

Emma pursed her lips. "How can you be so charitable to one who hurt you so? I suppose I should be cast down at the thought of him killed in battle, and indeed I am very sorry for Lady Dayton's sake. But I shall never be able to forgive Hugh—*Lieutenant* Warrilow"— she said on seeing Lucy open her mouth to speak —"for how he hurt my dearest sister." She reached a hand to Lucy's face, brushing her gloved thumb over her cheek.

Lucy's cheeks were rosy again now, even without rouge. They hadn't always been, though. For so long after Hugh Warrilow's departure, her face had been pale, wan, and thinner than usual.

Lucy frowned. "You are much too critical of him, Emma."

She always looked grave when Emma spoke her mind about Hugh Warrilow.

"He is a good, kind man," Lucy said, "much better than you give him credit for. And I harbor him no ill-will." She inclined her head.

"To be sure, it is not a time of my life I should ever choose to repeat, but"— she put a hand up to silence Emma's retort —"I shouldn't wish to have married him, knowing he was so opposed to it."

"You were *engaged*, Lucy," Emma said, setting her empty glass down on the tray held by a passing footman.

"Not officially," Lucy said. "We never courted." She shook her head. "It was not official."

Emma shrugged her shoulders. "It may as well have been. Everyone knew that you were meant to wed."

Lucy paused before answering. "Yes. But that was no fault of his. Besides, he received punishment enough from friends and acquaintances afterward. Including you." She looked Emma in the eye with a hint of censure.

Lucy had not been at all thrilled upon discovering that Emma had given him the cut direct after everything had happened. No matter how devastated she had been to learn that her love was unrequited and that she was not to marry him after all, Lucy had been a staunch defender of Hugh Warrilow.

Emma would never understand it. Nor could she find it in herself to regret what she had done. She could hardly have stood up to dance with the man who had just shattered Lucy's heart and then dared to show up to a ball—all while Lucy was too devastated to get out of bed.

Emma would have done anything to take on Lucy's heartache in her stead.

"Well," Emma said, perking up, "I am sure that—if he *is* alive—he is kicking himself for having turned down the opportunity to marry a woman with a heart as kind and good as yours. That you have forgiven him says nothing at all about him but *everything* good about you, my sweet Lucy."

"Much as you pretend that it is not the case," Lucy said, "*you* have the more loyal and kind heart between the two of us, Emma."

"Bah," Emma said, holding her chin up with feigned hauteur, "my heart has nothing to say to anything."

"Perhaps," Lucy said hesitantly, "that is only because you have not yet found the gentleman it responds to."

"Then I hope I never shall. I shall marry for convenience or not at all, Lucy."

"And that is why you are accepting the attentions of Mr. Douglas?"

"Yes," Emma said baldly.

"But you have nothing at all in common," said Lucy, an almost pleading note to her voice.

"*That* is precisely why his suit is appealing. I shan't have to worry about one of us falling in love with the other. Both of us are reasonable, neither given to romantics; I think we shall suit well enough."

Emma's eyes sought out Mr. Douglas, who had removed his mask entirely and was standing beside his younger sister. He was a very practical man, as was demonstrated by the neat clothing visible underneath his equally-plain domino.

It was something Emma appreciated about him, as she glanced around the room at the vibrant waistcoats, intricate cravats, and high collars, many of which were beginning to wilt due to the warmth of the ball. Unless one stood near one of the windows where a frigid breeze blew in from outside, the humid heat generated by candles, fires, and dozens of bodies in the ballroom was stifling. Emma's hooded domino only added to the oppressive heat.

She was very much looking forward to a respite from the unending string of balls and parties they had been attending in anticipation of Parliament's holiday recess.

Lucy heaved a sigh. "Is it wrong of me to say, Emma, that I want more for you than Mr. Douglas?"

Emma saw Lucy's eyes on the man and suddenly felt defensive. It was unlike Lucy to say anything uncomplimentary. She could find it in her to defend the man who had jilted her, but she could find nothing good to say of Mr. Douglas?

"Wanted more for me?" Emma said. "What more? My own Mr. Pritchard? My own version of Hugh Warrilow to jilt me?"

Lucy was silent, and Emma glanced at her with a stab of guilt. She squeezed her eyes shut. "I am sorry, Lucy. That was terribly cruel. Please forgive me. I think that this heat has made me irritable. You know that I have never had a great interest in marrying." She smiled wryly. "I only entertain the notion now because I overheard Mrs. Richins claiming that I couldn't convince a shopkeeper to offer for me now that I am on the shelf. Naturally I must prove her wrong."

Lucy was in too grave a humor to laugh at Emma's jest, and Emma took her hand. "What do you say to this, Lucy? If Mr. Douglas doesn't come up to scratch and offer for me, I give you leave to choose my husband for me."

Lucy smiled weakly, looking Emma in the eye. "You were meant to love deeply, Emma. I just know it. It is why I am saddened at the prospect of you marrying without any affection at all."

Emma sighed. "Oh Lucy, I don't have a heart like yours. I think you would love any person you married. *Your* heart holds enough warmth to make up for the coldness of mine."

Lucy shook her head emphatically, her ringlets, swaying to and fro. "Your heart is anything but cold—I know that better than anyone. You may not give your heart easily, but once given, it is secure. It is what I love so much about you: I never need doubt you."

Emma squeezed Lucy's hand. "That last part, at least, is true."

It was too like Lucy to believe the best of everyone. It was what had allowed her to forgive Hugh Warrilow so readily. But Lucy's tendency to think the best of every person she encountered was what had resulted in her heart being broken.

And though she might sometimes envy Lucy's optimism, Emma felt more secure, more able to protect Lucy from further pain by being the more practical and realistic of the two.

It was that pragmatism that led her to desire a marriage of convenience.

Lucy might not be satisfied with Emma marrying Mr. Douglas, but Emma was perfectly content with her decision. Or at least tolerably so.

2

Hugh fiddled with the gold carnelian signet ring in his hand as the carriage wheels rumbled over the uneven dirt road. Aside from the ache in his shoulder, he hardly noticed the jolting—he had experienced far worse during the war. But the cold did seem to aggravate his mending wound—and England felt colder than he remembered it being when he had last stepped foot on its shores a few years ago.

He looked down at the ring, turning it so that the fading light through the chaise window glinted on the red stone—a red he knew too well. It was the same color that had saturated his clothes and his skin on the battlefield. It had been days before the remnants had disappeared from under his nails—a reminder of how tightly he had clutched at Seymour's clothing as his life slipped away before Hugh's eyes.

He closed his fingers around the ring, clenching his fist and his jaw as he looked through the window, scanning the countryside. Anything to turn his mind from those images.

For a moment, he had considered taking the road that led to the Seymours' home in order to deliver the signet ring to Mrs. Seymour—

perhaps the last remnant of her husband she would see. But as the carriage had drawn closer to the crossroad, Hugh's nerves had failed him.

Would Mrs. Seymour blame him? She could hardly do so more than Hugh blamed himself. How would he bear seeing her grief? How would he bear it, knowing that, if it weren't for him, her husband would very likely still be alive?

He wasn't ready to face Mrs. Seymour. But would he ever be ready?

Tucking the ring into the small pocket of his waistcoat, he consoled himself with the fact that an unanticipated visit at the dinner hour would hardly be welcome. It would have to wait for another day.

He tapped his fingers on his leg nervously. When he had begun the journey home from Spain, he had comforted himself with the knowledge that he would have plenty of time to steel himself to the prospect of facing his family.

But he was here—home again—and no more confident of the reception he would receive. He had to hope that his mother, at least, would rejoice in seeing him.

But nothing was certain. Much could change over the course of three years, and Hugh had provided plenty of reason for resentment by his long silence.

He had been nothing but a disappointment. And yet she had never made him feel like one. She was the person he had most regretted leaving when his uncle had bought him a commission.

Of course, he had also regretted leaving his brother Alfred behind.

And Emma, too. But that was a train of thought he knew better than to follow and encourage. That was all in the past. It was better to leave it well enough alone.

Hugh glanced out the window and sighed, easily recognizing their location, even with the fast-falling snow. They had almost reached the road to Marsdon House—another errand he would need to accomplish before long.

How he would face Lucy and the Caldwells after what he put them through, he had no idea. But he had to. It was time to make things right—or as right as he could.

And as for Emma? His short encounter with her had raised more questions than Hugh had answers to.

He shook his head, wishing it could shake his feelings away. His attachment to Emma was something he had vowed to rid himself of. It couldn't be permitted to interfere with his aim. It was that attachment which had landed him in this whole mess in the first place.

Soon enough, the hired chaise rolled to a stop, and the lights of Norfield streamed through the carriage window, beckoning Hugh home. He sat still for a moment, scanning the façade of the house, masked by the thick flakes falling to the ground. It was the dinner hour—perhaps not the ideal conditions for an unanticipated return. But what *would* be ideal conditions?

Hugh noted the other carriage in the courtyard with a grimace. Visitors. They would certainly get more than they had bargained for in coming to Norfield tonight, witnessing his return. Whoever it was, they would have quite an ordeal driving home, if it were possible at all. Visibility would be terrible, not to mention the state of the roads.

He took in a deep breath. It was time.

Supporting all his belongings with his uninjured arm, he passed by the path to the front door, opting instead for a side door which would allow him to avoid the inevitably shocked reaction of the servants.

Cringing as the side door creaked, he peeked his head inside before slipping in and setting his bags lightly on the floor. They could be retrieved later.

He blew a breath through his lips, straightened his shoulders, and walked down the corridor to the dining room, feeling strangely at home and simultaneously out of place.

The clanking of silverware sounded within the dining room, and the smell of hollandaise sauce—likely over a brace of pheasants, if his father's tastes hadn't changed—wafted under the door.

The servants would still be within, along with whatever visitors, a fact Hugh didn't relish. But there was no helping it.

He pulled the door open and took a step inside. All the ambient noise ceased immediately, accompanied by the sight of forks suspended mid-air and jaws hanging agape.

Hugh's eyes found his mother first. She was blinking—slow prolonged blinks—as if each one might change what she was seeing.

"Mama," he said, striding toward her and kneeling by her side, swallowing his anxiety as he reached for her hand.

She was frozen in place, staring at him rigidly until her hand flew to her mouth to stifle a sob. Scooting her chair back from the table, she rose, pulling Hugh up with her, and threw her arms around him. The pain that shot through his right arm was worth it—to be able to hold and be held by her after such a long time.

"How?" she said in his ear.

"So, the prodigal returns," came the voice of Hugh's father. He sat in his chair, his wrists resting on the edge of the table, a hard set to his jaw.

"I believe," said Hugh's brother Alfred, standing and striding over to Hugh with a large grin on his face, disbelief in his eyes, and his arms outstretched, "that in the parable, the father sees his son from a long way off, which quite obviously none of us did. What a welcome surprise, though!"

In the parable, the father also ran to meet his son, falling on his son's neck and kissing him. But Hugh knew his father too well to expect any such welcome from him.

He released his mother with a quick, soft kiss on her cheek.

"Alfred," he said in a gruff voice, clapping his good arm around his younger brother.

"We had given you up for dead, Hugh," Alfred said. "I should have known you wouldn't be such easy prey for the French."

Hugh chuckled and gripped Alfred's shoulder. "I have missed you."

He stepped back, his gaze travelling curiously over the face of an unfamiliar young woman who looked at him with curiosity, and then he froze.

Emma Caldwell sat rigid in her chair, her nostrils flared.

What in the world was she doing at Norfield? Hugh shut his open mouth.

The gray eyes which had unknowingly looked at him a few nights ago now bored into him.

Hugh swallowed. How did she manage to look so beautiful even in a rage? Her mask the other night had hidden enough from him that he'd been blissfully ignorant of how it affected him to see her. Still. All these years later.

It was not a welcome realization.

He looked at his mother who looked a nervous apology at him. "Emma is here on her way to Marsdon House, but she kindly stopped to convey a gift and her father's congratulations to Alfred and Miss Bolton."

"Congratulations?" Hugh said, swallowing the large knob in his throat and looking to Alfred.

The tense look on Alfred's face transformed into a smile. "Miss Bolton has done me the honor of accepting my offer of marriage." He looked to Miss Bolton with an almost foolishly joyful grin.

Hugh clapped him on the back again. "I felicitate you both. What wonderful news!"

"It is indeed," his mother said, but she was watching Emma and grimacing in understanding at her. "I apologize, my dear." She sent Hugh a helpless glance.

Emma set down her utensils slowly and deliberately. "Don't apologize, Lady Dayton. I think it best that I leave, though, and leave you to your reunion. It was lovely to see you"— she looked to Miss Bolton —"and to meet *you*, Miss Bolton. I hope you know how pleased my father was to learn of your engagement—he thinks himself the most fortunate godfather in the world and was very anxious for me to deliver you his congratulations. I, too, wish you both very well. We all do."

"But you have hardly eaten," Hugh's mother said.

"I have a small appetite," Emma replied with a polite smile. She gently pushed her chair back, and the footman behind rushed to assist her. Her gaze flitted to Hugh and then to the door.

Something shifted inside of Hugh and he blinked twice, realizing what was happening. "No, Miss Caldwell, please. Have a seat. I will go."

Emma looked at him for a moment with a measuring gaze, then shook her head, heading for the door.

He stared straight ahead, clenching his fists. How could she still harbor so much hate toward him? It was as if no time had passed. He cleared his throat. "A journey home in this weather would be folly, Miss Caldwell."

She turned her head to look at him, hesitating on the threshold where a footman held the door open for her.

Hugh walked over to one of the tall windows, pulling back the curtains. The sun was down, but the landscape glowed with the reflective light of the snow in the air and on the ground.

Emma bit her lip and then straightened her shoulders. "Thank you for your concern"— was there a bite to the words? —"but I imagine my coachman can handle a matter of a few short miles."

"Only if he is a fool," Hugh said, fighting the irritation he felt at knowing she would rather risk her life than spend another minute under the same roof. He took in a breath to stabilize his emotions. "I barely made it here myself, and the snow has only worsened since then."

"Please, dear," Lady Dayton said softly. "Reconsider. I could never forgive myself if you came to harm on the way home. You have your belongings with you, don't you? You *must* stay."

"Indeed," came the soft voice of Miss Bolton, "I cannot think it wise to go out in such weather. Do stay."

Emma was silent for a moment, her jaw clenching and unclenching. She looked at Lady Dayton, then shut her eyes briefly and sighed. "Very well," she said, moving back to her seat.

The footman closed the door.

Hugh nodded at them all. "I bid you all a good night." He turned toward the door, which the footman rushed to open.

"Sit down." The voice of Hugh's father wasn't raised, but Hugh recognized the authority in it—the authority he had come to know best when he had flouted it by refusing to marry Lucy.

He paused, struggling within himself. He had become accustomed to receiving orders during the war as well as to giving them. It was Emma's presence that made him hesitate to follow these particular orders, though. To follow them would be to cause her discomfort and to subject himself to her fulminating glances all evening.

But what did it matter? Nothing he could say or do would change her opinion of him. To defy his father would be to court his ire unnecessarily, and all the while, Emma would remain angry with him whether or not he stayed.

His stomach growled, and he breathed in the scent of roast duck —his favorite dish. He hadn't eaten it in years, at least not the way that the Warrilow's chef Pudston prepared it.

He turned back toward the table, noting with a tensing of his jaw that the only seat open was the one opposite Emma. Judging from the way she inhaled through flared nostrils, she had noticed the same thing.

He made his way over to the chair and sat, busying himself with his napkin and then with serving himself from the food in front of him—never mind that it was a dish he had never liked.

An uncomfortable silence reigned for a time, until Hugh's father spoke.

"Hugh, do you intend to go to London when Parliament resumes? Or is this a leave of absence?"

Hugh cleared his throat and finished chewing. "I haven't decided yet. It will depend upon a few matters that are outside of my control."

He suppressed a desire to glance at Emma, wondering what she would think if she had known of his intent to ask for Lucy's hand in marriage. No doubt she would do her best to persuade Lucy to refuse him. "I am technically on leave. But if my shoulder heals fully, I may well return to my regiment. As it currently can't bear the weight of a saber, though, I am wholly useless for the time being."

His father continued cutting his food, and he didn't look at Hugh when he said, "We should prepare ourselves, then, for another sudden departure, I suppose."

There was a hard note to his voice, and Hugh watched Alfred's hand slow as he set his glass down. He didn't meet Hugh's gaze, and Hugh's brows knit. The joyous expression Alfred had been wearing had waned, and in its place was something more like a frown.

The short two years between Hugh and Alfred had resulted in a strong fraternal bond—one of mutual respect and affection. Alfred's joy upon seeing Hugh had been genuine, his embrace making Hugh's shoulder ache with its force. What was this frown, then?

His father's reaction to his return, on the other hand, had been expected, apathetic as it was. He had never been the demonstrative type, and Hugh had known very well that in leaving to join the army, his father considered him to be abandoning his duties as heir. It was only natural he would be upset upon Hugh's return, particularly after the silence he had subjected them to.

Emma was watching him, an almost amused expression in her eyes. She held his gaze for a moment, the amusement turning to a hard challenge, before reaching for a nearby dish. Was she glad to see his father chastise him for his behavior? Of course, she must believe he deserved every bit of it. She had made it abundantly clear what she thought of him.

"No, Father," Hugh said. "You have no need to fear that. My joining the army was rash and disrespectful. I am very sorry for my behavior and for not keeping you informed of my circumstances or my intent to come home."

Out of the corner of his eye, Hugh saw Emma go still.

He reached for his glass, his throat feeling suddenly dry. He had intended to apologize to his parents from the time he had decided to come home, but he had not intended to do it at the dinner table with guests present—particularly not someone as antagonistic toward him as Emma.

It was difficult to say the words—to acknowledge aloud that he had acted like a coward in refusing to marry Lucy and then in joining the army so suddenly. At the time, he had told himself that accepting his uncle's offer to buy a commission was a worthy cause, that it was the only way to recoup his honor, to demonstrate his courage and character.

And he *had* done much of that during his years fighting for England. He knew what kind of man he wanted to be now.

But it didn't change the fact that there was an added benefit to his departure: not having to remain among his acquaintances to face the consequences of his actions.

Well, he must face them now, whatever they might be.

WHEN HE ENTERED the drawing room behind his father and Alfred, Hugh spotted Emma seated by the fire, a shawl lying across her knees and an unfocused look in her eyes.

She was unlikely to welcome conversation with him, but Hugh knew that he needed to apologize to her. He had anticipated having more time before attempting it—he hadn't even been sure she would give him the opportunity to speak to her, given her behavior toward him three years ago—but it made little sense to wait. Waiting would give him time to rethink. It was better to act now while he was feeling brave enough.

He straightened his shoulders and walked to the vacant chair near her, taking a seat on the plush cushion. The luxuries of life at home were strange to him.

Emma was staring into the fire, the light from the dancing flames reflected in her eyes, but she turned her head as Hugh sat down, a long, patience-pleading blink telling him that his presence was—as he had expected—not gladly received.

"Miss Caldwell," he said. "I realize that there is likely no other gentleman in this country whose company you have less desire of, so I shan't take much of your time."

Her gaze flicked toward him. Was there a softening in her eyes? He remembered a time when her eyes hadn't looked at him with such severity—when they hadn't reminded him so much of steel; when he'd had a sliver of hope, at least, that someday she might return his regard.

She said nothing, though, returning her gaze to the fire.

He swallowed. Three years away, and she still had such influence on his pulse. Whether his nerves were due to her cold behavior or rather evidence that his regard for her was intact was unclear.

If there was any mercy in the world, it would be the former. He knew what he needed to do, but he would much rather do it without romantic regard for Emma complicating things. He had given his attachment to her far too much importance in the past. He understood now that duty needed to transcend emotion.

And marriage was certainly his duty.

"I wish to apologize," he said.

Emma let out a small scoffing noise.

Hugh persisted. "I wish to apologize for my behavior toward Lucy. It was abominable." Meeting only silence, he continued, "While I intended no ill toward her, the effect of my actions was the same as if I had."

He clasped his hands together, looking at the small, fading scars from the battles he had fought, from the thorny bushes he had run through during the campaigns he had participated in. In many ways, that had all been easier than confronting Emma and admitting his faults. "I understand that she suffered greatly, and I know you care for her enough that you must have suffered along with her. I don't expect forgiveness"— Emma's head turned toward him —"but I wish you to know that I regret having caused so much pain. I hope that I may live to right some of my wrongs."

Emma's eyes had calmed, he thought, until his last words. Her body drew back.

"And how do you intend to accomplish such a feat?"

Hugh rubbed his lips together with a sudden, vexing doubt about the merits of his plan. "I hope," he said, choosing his words with care, "that your sister will allow me the opportunity to demonstrate that."

Emma blinked. "I don't think I understand."

Hugh shifted in his seat. She was going to force him to say it. "I hope to speak with your father regarding my intentions before saying any more on the subject."

Emma stared at him. "Surely you jest."

Hugh rubbed a hand down his pant leg. Emma was not one to mince words—it was one of her best qualities, but just now it gave him the desire to loosen his cravat. He had never felt more uncomfortable, had never felt that his character was less satisfactory.

"I am in earnest, Miss Caldwell." It was all he could manage.

A humorous light entered Emma's eyes, and she pursed her lips. "I suppose I could leave you to discover how things stand on your own—it is an enticing prospect, I admit." She shook her head. "But no, it is not what Lucy would wish." She clasped her hands in her lap and reclined in her chair, watching Hugh. "Lucy is engaged to be married."

Hugh's mouth opened and shut. He had learned on arrival in England that Lucy was still unmarried, but how had he not considered that she might be engaged?

As he looked at Emma, who seemed to be mildly enjoying his discomfiture, his assumption that Lucy would still be unmarried seemed presumptuous at best and offensive at worst.

"I must ask," Emma said, "did you expect that she would wait for your return? After you jilted her and made her the talk of the town for weeks?"

Her words were harsh. But he didn't fault her for them. He

deserved them. And though it saddened him to hear confirmation of what Emma thought of him, he could imagine that her words were borne of grief for her sister's suffering—grief which manifested as anger toward him.

When he spoke, his voice was soft. "It does sound ridiculous now that I hear you say it. I imagine I sound like a coxcomb."

"Aren't you?"

His head whipped up, and he saw the teasing glint in her eyes— just enough to soften the insult. He let out a small laugh. "It would appear so."

He would gladly take teasing jibes at his expense over frigid animosity.

"I am pleased to hear that she is to marry," he said. "I wish her great happiness."

He nodded to her and stood, feeling a weight off his shoulders.

He hadn't approached marriage to Lucy thinking himself a martyr, for she was a kind, agreeable young woman. But he *had* known some hesitation, and it was certainly duty rather than any particular warmth of feeling which had propelled the intention to offer for her.

But seeing Emma at the masquerade and now again, sitting at the dining room table in his childhood home—her presence had hit him with a force reminiscent of the one that had lodged a bullet in his shoulder a few months ago.

She was every bit the engaging, artless woman he had loved in secret for years.

Except when she spoke with him.

3

Emma straightened her neck as Lieutenant Warrilow walked away, having bid her a good night and rejoined his mother across the room.

The fire crackled in the grate before her, and she suddenly felt too warm. She shifted her legs away from the flames and stared at the brocade curtains hanging at the windows, even though she knew a desire to observe Lieutenant Warrilow more.

She had thought she would never see him again. Nor had she wanted to see him. But being confronted with him so suddenly at dinner—with his snow-speckled hair and his broad shoulders, accentuated by his brown great coat—she had determined to treat him with as much cold indifference as she could muster.

Lucy, with her generous heart, might be able to forgive him, but Emma couldn't see him without thinking of how Lucy had shut herself in her room for hours, refusing to talk to anyone, upon discovering that he had no intention of marrying her.

But Emma's plan to make it clear that he was not forgiven had been somewhat rattled by his forthright admission of wrong. He had taken the wind out of her sails when he had said he had no expectation of being forgiven, when he had softly acknowledged that, in hurting Lucy, he had hurt her family as well.

She could hardly throw his wrongs in his face after such behavior.

She glanced over at him, seated on the arm of the chair his mother occupied. He was peering over his mother's shoulder at the sheets of music she held, one of his hands resting on her shoulder as he smiled down at her in an exchange of words.

Lady Dayton looked up at him as though he were her greatest gift and accomplishment. There was no trace of resentment in the woman.

Could Emma forgive him as completely as his mother had?

She looked away. Forgive and forget—those words were always paired together, but Emma could hardly forget what he had put Lucy through.

She stood, walking to the window. The blackness of the late evening couldn't obscure the large, white flakes falling to the ground.

Leaning against the cold window frame, she sighed. It was difficult to tell just how much snow had fallen, but she had to believe life wouldn't be so cruel as to keep her at Norfield longer than one night.

She turned as she saw Lady Dayton approach.

Lieutenant Warrilow walked over to the fireplace, leaning a hand on the mantel above as he stared into the flames, moving the wood with the poker.

Lady Dayton came and stood shoulder-to-shoulder with Emma, the skin beside her eyes wrinkling as she smiled warmly.

"I know that this is not at all what you bargained for, my dear," she said, her eyes flicking over to Lieutenant Warrilow as she tucked her arm into Emma's. "And it is particularly unfair when you came to do such a good deed. Your father has been a wonderful godfather to Alfred."

Emma laughed softly. "He takes his duties very seriously. He is more likely to be considered an over-involved godfather than an unconcerned one." Her smile faded as her eyes landed on Lieutenant

29

Warrilow, still prodding at the logs within the grate. What was he thinking about with such a furrowed brow?

"I am happy to spend more time with *you*, in any case," Emma said, turning to look at Lady Dayton. "I imagine you are elated to have him home."

Lady Dayton smiled and sighed contentedly. "Yes, though I believed at first that my eyes were deceiving me. I haven't felt such joy in years." She turned to Emma, and her brows drew inward. "I know it pains you to be in his presence, and I am only sorry that my joy must necessarily include your suffering."

Emma squeezed Lady Dayton's arm. "Nonsense. You needn't worry about me."

"But I do," she said, and her eyes returned to her son. "I worry about both of you."

Emma pursed her lips. Lieutenant Warrilow hardly looked like the type of person one needed worry over. Those broad shoulders and powerful arms seemed more than capable of carrying their own burdens. "Worry about his injury, you mean?"

As if to confirm Emma's question, Lieutenant Warrilow winced and put back the poker, bringing a hand to his shoulder and rubbing it.

"A bit," Lady Dayton replied with a worried frown. "More than his physical wounds, though, I worry about the other wounds he carries."

Emma was silent. She wished to commiserate with Lady Dayton, to comfort her. But she found it difficult when the object of compassion was someone who had behaved so deplorably.

"He entered the war wounded, in many ways," Lady Dayton said, watching him, "and I know that he must have experienced even worse in battle. I believe he entered the army as a form of penance." She turned her head to Emma. "For what he did to Lucy."

Emma controlled her face as much as she could. She had always assumed that his abrupt departure had been a coward's way out of the stir he had caused. Was she wrong? Or was his mother simply inclined, as all mothers were, to believe the very best of her son?

If the latter, Emma couldn't fault her for it. It was what one liked in Lady Dayton—she was always charitable in her reading of character. Emma came away from her company wishing to be better and do better, if only to live up to the image Lady Dayton seemed to have of her.

"Well," Emma said, "surely nothing is more likely to heal his wounds—physical or otherwise—than spending the holidays with you."

Lady Dayton put a hand on Emma's. "Perhaps it will do Hugh good to spend time in your company, as well. I know he has great respect for you."

Emma blinked rapidly, her eyes flitting to him. He was speaking with Miss Bolton, the grave tilt to his brow gone.

Hugh Warrilow respected Emma? What had she given him to respect? She had been nothing but unkind to him since he had made it clear that he didn't intend to marry Lucy.

Emma had liked him well enough before that, to be sure. They had found themselves in opposition to one another on a number of occasions during childhood, but nothing outside of the ordinary disagreements and quarrels between girls and boys who play together.

"You look surprised, my dear," said Lady Dayton with a note of humor.

Emma's eyebrows shot up. "Well, yes. That's because I *am* surprised."

Lady Dayton turned toward her and regarded her with narrowed, searching eyes. "You *don't* know, then," she said with wonder.

Emma drew back slightly. "I don't know what?"

Lady Dayton's eyes moved to her son once again, and she pursed her lips, as if trying to decide whether or not she should voice her thoughts. She sighed and smiled at Emma. "Nothing, my dear."

Emma was too bewildered to respond. And since Lord Dayton

came shortly after to escort his wife to bed, Emma was left to wonder at Lady Dayton's meaning.

WHEN EMMA WOKE in the morning, she was grateful to see the fire lit in her grate. Even with its warmth, she pulled the covers more tightly around her for a few minutes before stepping out of bed and shivering. The fire provided heat to the immediate area around it, but the further away she was, the more her skin prickled in the icy air.

She rang the bell and searched her portmanteau for a shawl, which she hurriedly wrapped around her shoulders before stepping toward the window curtains and pulling them back.

The sight was dazzling. Through the ice crystals which clung to the tall window pane, Emma could see a landscape blanketed in white—the hedgerows which lined the drive to Norfield were one, undefined mass of billowing snow clouds; the trees sagged under the weight of their burden, periodically dropping streams of glittering powder onto the snow beneath.

The undisturbed quality of the view struck her until she realized what it likely meant. The roads wouldn't be passable. Not even for the short distance she needed to cover to arrive at Marsdon House.

She sighed and slumped against the window sill, drawing back again as the frozen glass pierced through all the layers she wore. She would have to trust that the sun would break through the clouds and melt the thick cloak of snow, though it seemed a shame to wish for such a thing. How many times had she and Lucy wished and prayed for snow during holidays past?

She smiled, remembering how they would pray at the bedside and then race to the window, looking up at the night sky as if their prayer might be immediately answered with a shower of white flakes.

Lucy would already have arrived at Marsdon House with Mr. Pritchard, and tomorrow would be Christmas Eve, the day Emma had been looking forward to for weeks. She closed her eyes and imagined the smell of the fresh garlands of greenery which would be strung up all over the house; the glowing light of the *Christbaum;* curling up in a blanket by the fire with Lucy; the intoxicating and cozy atmosphere.

She couldn't bear to miss it.

She opened her eyes and stared at the scene outside, sighing resignedly. She hardly had a say in the matter.

DRESSED in her favorite white muslin dress and with the India shawl her mother had given her wrapped around her shoulders, Emma walked down the wide staircase to the sitting room later that morning. There was only one occupant within: Miss Bolton. She sat in a chair nearest the fireplace, reading a book. One of her chestnut curls bounced as she looked up to see Emma.

"Miss Caldwell," she said with a smile. "Good morning."

Emma returned the greeting and hesitated for a moment, trying to decide which seat to take.

"Do come sit," Miss Bolton said, indicating the chair opposite hers. "I don't remember the last time it was so cold, and these seats provide the best chance at warming up."

Emma took her seat in the green, velvety chair, letting out a breath as the heat of the licking flames spread over her body. "It is very cozy, isn't it? Such a comfort to have a fire's warmth when the world outside is covered in snow and ice." She let out a little laugh. "I would be thrilled if I didn't despair of ever getting home."

"I hope you shan't dislike it," Miss Bolton said in a shy voice, "if I confess that I am a little pleased that you are held hostage here by the weather." She smiled sheepishly. "I am glad not to be the only guest."

Emma laughed softly. "I am flattered! But Lord and Lady Dayton never make one feel anything but perfectly at home, in my experience."

Miss Bolton's eyes widened. "Oh, yes! To be sure, they are

nothing but kind and welcoming. Lady Dayton is so very gracious. And though I hadn't known to expect Lieutenant Warrilow, I find him to be very affable and obliging, besides his return being the most unexpected surprise for Alfred."

Emma cleared her throat and inclined her head with a forced smile.

Miss Bolton tilted her head and bit her lip, regarding Emma for a moment. "Perhaps it is too forward of me, but"— she lowered her book onto her lap, —"it seems that you and the lieutenant are not on good terms. May I ask why?"

Emma's mouth opened and then closed, and her eyes narrowed. "You aren't familiar with the history between him and my sister, then? I thought everyone knew."

Miss Bolton shook her head. "But I am only just out, you know, so I am naturally ignorant of many things that happened before my arrival in town."

Emma adjusted her shawl, stalling for time. How much should she tell Miss Bolton? It seemed unfair to speak ill of Lieutenant Warrilow when they were guests of his family, under the same roof as him. Besides, Miss Bolton had made it clear that she thought well of the lieutenant after their short acquaintance. Emma might be angry with the lieutenant, but she wouldn't stoop to sullying his reputation with his future sister-in-law.

"He seems far too kind," Miss Bolton said with a wrinkled brow, "to have done some of the terrible things I have heard of men doing— killing each other in duels at dawn and the like." She shivered.

"No, nothing like that," Emma said, shifting in her seat as she recalled how she had demanded that her brother challenge Lieu-tenant Warrilow to a duel. Looking back, she was relieved that he had not complied with the demand. She suspected that Lieutenant Warrilow was a fine shot, while her brother was several years his junior and hardly a sportsman—he had much more of a turn for liter-ature and education.

Emma looked at Miss Bolton, whose eyes watched her with

curiosity. If she refused to indulge her, Miss Bolton could easily discover the state of things from someone else. It was only a matter of time until she knew, and perhaps it was better that she hear it from someone near to Lucy.

"The lieutenant and my sister were meant to marry—an understanding between our families since childhood—but Lieutenant Warrilow decided against the match." She shut her mouth tightly, refusing to allow the melodramatic words *"leaving my sister to nearly die of a broken heart"* to escape her lips.

Miss Bolton's posture relaxed, and her eyes glazed over for a moment. "But why?" she said.

Emma suddenly felt impatient. How could she respond to that question? Saying that the lieutenant was selfish? Unsympathetic? A coward? "I am sure only he could answer that."

Miss Bolton looked troubled, as though she needed to reconcile what she was learning with the gentleman she had met the night before. "I am sure there must be some reason."

A floorboard creaked, and Miss Bolton jumped in her chair.

Lieutenant Warrilow stood in the doorway, a disturbed look in his eyes, which were fixed on Emma.

Her cheeks grew warm, and a glance at Miss Bolton's red face confirmed that she, too, was mortified to be discovered in this particular discussion. Emma knew a desire to clarify that it had been Miss Bolton's curiosity which had led to the conversation and not any malevolent desire on Emma's part to speak of the lieutenant's behavior to strangers.

"Breakfast awaits," the lieutenant said.

Unable to bear another moment of silent embarrassment, Emma stood, one side of her shawl dropping down her arm in her haste to stand up. She picked it up, arranged it quickly about her shoulder, and nodded at Miss Bolton. "I think I shall go to the breakfast room."

She felt her heart pick up speed as she neared the doorway where Lieutenant Warrilow still stood. He inclined his head and opened the door wider for her.

"Good morning, Miss Caldwell."

"Good morning," she replied, slipping past him and into the corridor. She took in a deep breath, only to realize that he was walking behind her and, soon enough, abreast of her.

"I shan't trouble you for long," he said, "but I wished to speak with you about your plans to continue to Marsdon House."

His voice had a sharp quality to it. Was it because he had overheard her and Miss Bolton? How much had he overheard, anyway?

"Yes?" she said.

"I hope you will not attempt it, Miss Caldwell."

She opened her mouth to speak, but he held up a hand. "I know that you likely wish to be anywhere but here, particularly at this time of year, but the temperatures have dropped dangerously. There is a thick layer of ice beneath all the snow you see." He indicated the snowy scene beyond the tall, frosted windows lining the corridor. "I shall endeavor to relieve you of my presence whenever possible, but I could never forgive myself if you came to harm attempting to travel these roads simply to avoid me."

Emma wrapped her shawl more tightly around her, feeling caught off guard by his direct acknowledgment of her sentiments. She laughed shakily. "What a character I should be to ask such a thing of you under your own roof."

"You haven't asked it of me," he said blankly. "But I believe I understand your sentiments well enough to conclude what you would wish."

She scoffed softly, turning to him and stopping. "What would you know of my sentiments? Or of anyone's sentiments but your own?" She bit her lip and swallowed, torn between defiance and embarrassment at her outburst.

His jaw clenched, but she thought she saw a flash of hurt in his eyes before he smiled wryly. "I don't believe anyone could be unaware of your sentiments toward me."

She thought of Lady Dutton's ball and the stricken look in Lieutenant Warrilow's eyes when she had ignored his request for a dance and walked away, leaving him mortified in front of dozens of people. She had felt justified at the time, her anger and desire to defend Lucy eclipsing any other consideration.

But now? Now she knew a small seed of doubt. Had she been too rash?

She seemed to be the only person who insisted upon continuing to punish Lieutenant Warrilow for his actions. Everyone else seemed to have moved past what he had done.

"Never mind that," he said softly, ending the silence between them. "I beg you not to leave until the roads are in a state fit for travel." He bowed to her and strode down the corridor, turning into the dining room.

Emma's brow wrinkled. She had assumed that they had a shared destination: the breakfast room.

Was he avoiding her?

Still feeling rattled from the encounter, she took in a deep breath and then exhaled before walking down the corridor to the breakfast room.

4

Hugh tapped his quill impatiently on the desk in front of him, looking out the library window where the landscape seemed to be frozen in time. He had attempted to open the front door earlier, but it was no use. The snow had piled in front of it and then hardened with the deep freeze of nighttime air. Beautiful though it might be, it was its own kind of prison.

Not since his injury had he felt so enclosed, unable to escape—stuck in the field hospital as he had been after the battle at Vitoria, with a raging fever, only to then spend weeks convalescing in the home of a Spanish family, hovering between life and death.

He certainly owed his life to the army surgeon who had retrieved the ball from his shoulder and to the Spanish doctor who had tended to him later. But at the time, in his more morose moments, he had often found himself wishing it had been him and not Seymour who had died on the battlefield.

Seymour had been with him from the beginning, since Hugh's first campaign, inspiring him with grit and determination, helping him forget the dark days behind him, and encouraging him when the opportunity for promotion to lieutenant presented itself. Hugh had even arranged for Seymour to join him in his new regiment. If he hadn't been so selfish and insisted on doing so, Seymour would very possibly still be alive.

A phantom pang shot through Hugh's shoulder.

Those were dark days after Seymour's death.

The door opened, and Alfred paused on the threshold, catching eyes with Hugh. Hugh smiled feebly, but he received no smile in return.

Alfred's jaw tensed, and Hugh's eyebrows snapped together.

"What is it?"

"Nothing," Alfred replied. "I didn't know you were in here. I will leave you."

"Come, Alfred," Hugh said, motioning to a chair nearby. "Have a seat. You have something you need to say to me. Come say it."

Alfred scoffed.

"What?" Hugh said, nonplussed.

Alfred shook his head. "Unbelievable. You come home after we haven't heard from you for a year—after even Mama has given you up for dead— and you immediately start ordering everyone and every-thing around?"

Hugh's jaw slackened, and his brows knit. Alfred's joy upon his unexpected arrival had only been eclipsed by their mother's joy. But it since seemed to have soured. Evidently Alfred had been laboring under strong emotions inside since their initial reunion.

Hugh had no response for his brother's words, only a tight feeling in his stomach. Had he made a mistake to come home? He had suspected that his family might be better off without him, and Alfred's behavior seemed to confirm that suspicion.

The silence lengthened, and Alfred began pacing the room, running his hand through his hair as Hugh watched.

"What have I done to upset you, Alfred? Whatever it was, it was certainly done unintentionally."

Alfred let out another scoffing noise. "Oh, nothing is ever intentional with you, is it, Hugh? You just can't help but harm everyone in the wake of your selfishness."

Hugh swallowed, weighed down by the sick feeling that descended into the pit of his stomach. It was not like Alfred to act this way—so resentful and angry. It must be more serious than Hugh had realized.

He leaned forward, staring at his interlocked fingers, and then looked up to say softly, "How have I harmed you, brother?"

Alfred stopped his pacing, turning to face Hugh, his anger morphing into a kind of helpless frustration. "Happy I am to have you home, Hugh, but this entire situation is unbearable. Miss Bolton accepted my offer of marriage, believing me to be the heir—her father believed me to be the heir. And now that I am not..." he trailed off, pulling at his hair as he looked up at the ceiling.

Hugh opened his mouth to respond, but what could he say? He stared down at his fingers again. His return had deprived Alfred of an inheritance he had come to believe belonged to him. And now he would have to clarify his changed fortunes to Miss Bolton's father.

"I am sorry, Alfred." It was all he could say. "It was thoughtless of me indeed not to anticipate how this all would affect you."

Alfred sighed. "How could you have known what was afoot?" He came and sat across from Hugh, staring wistfully to the windows. "I love her, Hugh. And I *had* her for a brief moment—I caught a glimpse of a future together." His brows drew together, and he dropped his head into his hands.

"You believe she will cry off when you explain your change in expectations?"

Alfred's head came up, his hair standing up in spots from him pulling at it. "She will. Her father will insist upon it. If you knew him, you would understand."

His look of dejection and hopelessness was pitiful. And yet Hugh could remember feeling something similar when he had realized that, in hurting her sister, he had ruined any small chance he had ever had with Emma.

Hugh rubbed his forehead. Why had he ever thought a return home to be his best course?

His desire to make reparations to Lucy was fruitless, engaged to be married as she was. His own brother saw his return as the greatest piece of misfortune that could have befallen him. And Emma...well, he had caused a resurfacing of her anger—and a painful reminder to himself of why he had refused to marry Lucy in the first place.

"You love Miss Bolton," Hugh said, determined to pull himself out of his unhappy thoughts. "She obviously returns your love. What if she still desires to marry you?"

"Then she would be a fool." The words were harsh. "She could do much better than me, Hugh. I as good as deceived her into accepting my proposal—at least her father will see it that way, and she is very much at his mercy. It would hurt her irreparably to be made to choose between him and me. I *must* release her from the engagement. And speak to Mr. Bolton." He closed his eyes and leaned back in his chair. "And the devil's in it that Miss Bolton is trapped here until the snow melts. Naturally, she cannot declare her desire to end the engagement when we are confined under the same roof for the foreseeable future."

Hugh straightened himself in his chair.

"Have you spoken to Miss Bolton about the situation?"

Alfred grimaced and nodded.

"And?"

"And she still holds out hope that her father will allow us to marry." He shook his head. "How I wish she were right."

Hugh looked out through the window and rubbed his chin. "Don't despair yet, Alfred. We will come about somehow if we but set our minds to it. I promise you that I will do everything in my power."

"You will help me?" Alfred said, a pleading look in his eyes.

Hugh stared at him and nodded decisively. There must be something he and Alfred could do to salvage things with Miss Bolton.

But what?

✳

HUGH PACED the gallery corridor upstairs, feeling his skin prickle. The gallery was always cold, but today it was miserably so.

He had weathered dinner with the family, Miss Bolton, and Emma, knowing that his presence was likely viewed by all but his mother as an unwelcome addition to what would have otherwise been a cheerful party.

Emma's eyes had seemed to find him a number of times over the course of the meal, and while they didn't smolder as they had done the night before, he was under no misapprehension about how she felt toward him.

At times, he had a pressing desire to explain himself to her; to help her understand that he had made an impossible choice; that he had chosen to hurt Lucy three years ago instead of disappointing her for a lifetime; that he had seen how Lucy had placed him on a pedestal that he had no business being on—one that he would inevitably fall from. And after the fall, he would have been forced to look into her disillusioned eyes.

He wanted to explain it all.

But it was no use. Emma wouldn't feel flattered to know of his love for her. She would only feel disgust. And he could bear her anger better than he could bear her disgust.

He paused in front of the portrait of his grandfather, clasping his hands behind him out of habit, just as he had always done in his grandfather's company. Even in the portrait, the man stood erect, grave, and precise—just as Hugh remembered him. *"A man is only as good as his word,"* he would always say. *"Better to lose one's life than to lose one's honor."*

Those words had reverberated in Hugh's mind night and day during his convalescence. He had hoped to regain in battle the honor he had lost by abandoning the marriage his family had hoped for. But instead, he had found himself holding his dying friend in his arms—a friend who had sacrificed his life to save Hugh; a friend without whom the ball in Hugh's shoulder would have been a ball in his chest.

Seymour had died to save a man with no honor; a man not worth saving.

Footsteps sounded down the corridor, muffled by the long gallery rug, and Hugh looked over, his swallow catching in his throat as his gaze met the form of Emma.

Hugh bowed. "Excuse me, Miss Caldwell," he said, moving to walk around her and out of the gallery.

His shoulder brushed hers as he rushed to pass her.

"Please stop," she said.

Hugh froze, then turned slowly. He didn't know if he had the energy to endure criticism from Emma at the moment. His grandfather's eyes had already condemned him enough.

She was looking at him, her hands clasped in front of her chest, thumbs fiddling.

"Have you absented yourself from the drawing room for my sake?" she said.

"It is no trouble," he said, inclining his head, forcing a smile, and then turning again to leave.

"It is quite unnecessary," she said, and he paused again.

What did she want from him? To force him to face his reprehensible actions by requiring him to face her anger?

She swallowed, and her chin came up slightly. "Surely we can manage to lay down our weapons in a temporary truce for Christmas."

He smiled wryly. What weapons did she believe him to be wielding? Surely his position was one of defense rather than attack.

"I don't wish," she continued, "to sully the season's memories for your family by causing a rift at a time of year where goodwill is meant to reign."

"So," he said slowly, the corners of his lips turned down in a thoughtful frown, "you wish to pretend to feelings you don't have?"

She gripped her lips together. "If you insist on describing it in such a manner."

He stared down into her eyes, scanning them. What was he to make of this offer? Was it an olive branch, however reluctantly offered? Or would it result in even greater resentment on her behalf, as her anger toward him festered under the pretense of civility? "How would *you* describe it?"

Her mouth twisted to the side, and she tried to suppress a smile.

"Pretending to feelings you don't have?" he suggested.

She laughed, and his muscles relaxed at the sight of her smile, his heart skipping at the sound of her laugh.

"I suppose so," she said.

He sighed. How would it feel to have Emma look at him with anything but spite?

"I have nothing to say against it," he said, "except that I harbor serious doubts that it is possible. For me, it would be easy." Too easy. "But for you?" He showed a mouth full of clenched teeth.

"You doubt my ability to act?" she said, her eyebrows up, ready to accept a challenge. "To smile and laugh in your company?"

He tilted his head and narrowed his eyes, staring down the long corridor beyond her. "Frankly, I do. It is easier to pretend to strong emotions where they do not exist than to pretend to less emotion than one truly feels." He knew it too well.

She looked at him without answering for a moment, and for the first time since he had arrived, he found himself wishing she would say whatever was on her mind. Because for the first time since he arrived, it wasn't glaringly obvious that her thoughts were uncharitable.

"I can manage it," she finally said. "It will set your mother's heart at ease if she sees that she doesn't have to worry about us quarreling—if she sees us on good terms. I see how it pains her not to have you near her solely because you are avoiding me. I don't wish to be the reason for that."

Hugh shrugged. "You must be the one to decide what you wish to do. I am happy to oblige if this is truly what you wish. And I will not hold it against you when your true feelings inevitably slip through."

"*When?*" she said, her brows shooting up and her mouth turning up in a smile both challenging and teasing. "You think me so unamiable that I cannot be perfectly civil for even a single day?"

He chuckled. Did she really think that it would only be one more day until the snow melted? "Not at all. You are amiable by nature." His smile flickered and began to fade. "It is only when you are near me that you are afflicted with disagreeableness."

She opened and then closed her mouth. "It wasn't always so."

"No, it was not," Hugh said, clenching his jaw and swallowing.

If the only image of her he'd had during his years away from home were the final one—the cold, haughty stare—he felt confident that his feelings would have quickly faded into nothing.

But more than that image, he had been haunted by memories from the more distant past; from the times he and Emma had danced or conversed with the carefree manner natural to two young people who had grown up in such proximity. He had watched the way her gray eyes brightened whenever she laughed, knowing that the only reason she could treat him with such familiarity had been because she was ignorant of his feelings for her. She had looked at him as a future brother-in-law, blissfully ignorant of the way his heart stuttered whenever she appeared.

"Well," she said, her voice still quiet and low, "then I shall simply have to draw on the past to assist me in our truce. I will have to pretend that"— she paused, her chin coming up determinedly —"that nothing ever happened."

Hugh only nodded, afraid to trust himself with saying anything more. The delicate scent of orange blossom perfume permeated the space they stood in—it was the same scent she had always worn, and it was faint enough that he was conscious of a wish to close the gap between them where it would be stronger

"If I am going to the trouble," she said, "of pretending that you are in my good graces, then *you* must promise not to wear such a grave expression all the time. Otherwise it will all be for nothing—your mother will know that something is still amiss."

He pursed his lips and tilted his head to the side. "Surely she will know once our truce has ended and your enmity is again on full display."

"Yes," she said matter-of-factly, "but by then I shall be home and can take care to avoid your company."

His nostrils flared briefly. Her words were anything but comforting. But it was probably for the best—for both of them—that she avoid his company. The dark hallway, her perfume, and the fact that they were alone together without any sparks flying—it gave him hope he had no right to feel.

Emma put her gloved hand out to him, a determined air about her.

Taking in a breath, he extended his arm in exchange, and they shook hands.

Her lips were drawn in a thin line, evidence of the difficulty she found in such a gesture.

His wry smile appeared. "Already you struggle."

Her mouth stretched into a smile, and Hugh's did the same in response. Had he not seen the expression that preceded it, had he not known the circumstances under which it occurred, he would have believed it to be a genuine smile. Apparently, he had underestimated her.

He, on the other hand, could already feel the way his heart twisted. Was he prepared for this? To be treated in a way much more reminiscent of their past relationship? It was a time when everything had been simpler.

But nothing was simple now. And a smile that hid malice was hardly something to rejoice over.

"You," she said in an accusatory tone, "seem to be struggling every bit as much as you believe I am. Surely you didn't forget how to smile during your time on the Continent?" Her eyes and mouth teased him, and his mouth felt dry.

He chuckled and smiled down at her, appreciating the way a dimple trembled on the right side of her mouth when she tried not to laugh.

Their eyes locked for a moment, and her smile wavered as her gaze traveled from his eyes down to his smile. She blinked rapidly and looked up at him again, as she swallowed and dropped his hand. His own hand hung in the air for a moment, tingling with the cool air and the memory of her touch.

"Good. You have not forgotten." Her tone was light and dispassionate, and she looked back down the corridor from the doorway she had come through. "Shall we go to the drawing room?"

He nodded, putting out his arm for her to take, wishing he knew what had caused her to look at him with such bewilderment. He was used to knowing precisely how she felt toward him—she had left no room for interpretation in the past.

How would he survive her counterfeit kindness?

When Emma awoke in the morning, she wrapped her dressing gown around herself and walked straight to the window. She had little hope that the snow would have melted enough overnight to allow her journey home, but she had to look, all the same.

Her lips parted in dismay as she looked out the window. A sheet of thick, white fog obscured the vista, and ice crystals clung to the window pane in a mesmerizing patchwork.

She heaved a resigned sigh. So, she would be spending Christmas Eve and Christmas at Norfield after all. Her stomach knotted as she thought about how worried her family must be. Surely they would be wondering if she had reached Norfield before the storm.

Today would have been the day they brought in the large, freshly cut Christmas tree and decorated it with paper flowers, fruit, and candles—a tradition the Caldwells had kept zealously in honor of Emma's German grandparents, Oma and Opa. Their love of the season had been well-preserved by Emma's mother, who had in turn fostered a love for it in her own children.

But with the frigid temperatures and the fog, would they even be able to carry on the tradition this year? It seemed such a shame that, when they finally had snow on Christmas Eve, there should be no tree to complete the vision Emma and Lucy had always hoped for—and that Emma should be absent entirely. Oma had been full of magical stories of Christmas in Germany and had always lamented the way the English went about things. She would be incensed to see how neglected her precious *Weihnachten* had become.

Emma smiled softly. She missed Oma's spirited personality and her descriptive stories which had made Emma feel as if she had been to Germany herself—as if she had smelled the cloves, the anise, the fruity scent of the *glühwein;* heard the rhythmic ringing of the bells; seen the flickering candles on the fir trees.

She shivered and stepped away from the window. As lamentable as her situation was—trapped at Norfield with the man she least wished to be trapped with—she was grateful that she had a fire in the grate and kind hosts. Had she left London two hours later, she might have been stuck in an inn with damp sheets, disagreeable fellow travelers, and terrible loneliness.

No, it was preferable to be where she was. And perhaps it wouldn't be as terrible as she had anticipated.

When she and Lieutenant Warrilow had walked into the drawing room the night before, her hand on his arm, Lady Dayton wasn't the only one who had looked on with mouth agape. All eyes were trained on them, Alfred's in particular, looking a question at Hugh.

Hoping to nip any possibility of someone verbalizing or questioning the abrupt change between them, Emma immediately addressed herself to Miss Bolton, successfully diverting attention from them and allowing her to remove her hand from the lieutenant's arm—where it still felt unnatural.

She hoped she had looked more confident than she had felt. It had taken no small degree of humility and courage to suggest the idea to Lieutenant Warrilow in the first place. After all, she had no desire to leave any room for doubt about what she thought of him.

49

But the knowledge that her feelings were depriving sweet Lady Dayton of her son's company, and seeing Lady Dayton's wistful glances at the door whenever he wasn't present—it had been too much for Emma. Her bitter behavior toward him felt much less like loyalty to Lucy and much more like selfishness—of whom the primary victim was Lady Dayton.

So she had determined to do what she could to ensure that Lady Dayton was able to enjoy her son's unexpected presence during the season instead of worrying about Emma's well-being.

But doubt had niggled at Emma since making her decision. Was she unintentionally giving Lieutenant Warrilow the idea that she had forgiven his behavior; that she had forgotten his treatment of Lucy?

Her only comfort was the relief and joy on Lady Dayton's face at the sight of them arm-in-arm.

Emma descended the stairs from her room with a small swallow. Why should she be nervous to see Lieutenant Warrilow? She simply needed to put aside her uncharitable feelings for a few days—to treat him as she had before everything had happened.

She raised her chin, stretched her mouth into a pleasant smile, and stepped down the last two stairs.

But Lieutenant Warrilow was the only one *not* in the breakfast parlor when she entered. She was conscious of a feeling of annoyance. Was he continuing to avoid her, despite their conversation the night before? He would give them away if he insisted upon doing so.

"Where is Hugh?" Lord Dayton said, looking around at the group as Emma took a seat. He reached for his cup of ale, mumbling, "Left us again, no doubt."

"Of course he hasn't," said Lady Dayton in a gentle voice. Her forehead creased. "I am not entirely sure where he went. He left with one of the servants, only saying that he would be gone a few hours."

Emma looked up from sipping her teacup. What in the world could he be doing? It was a veritable tundra outside.

"Went?" said Alfred, looking as perplexed as Emma felt. "You mean to say that he went outside? In this weather?"

Lady Dayton nodded. "Yes, though it took nearly ten minutes for the two of them to force the front door open."

Alfred scoffed. "Surely he wouldn't attempt driving on these roads. He must be mad!"

Lady Dayton shook her head, taking a moment to swallow her tea before answering. "I don't believe he took the carriage."

Alfred stared at his mother for a moment, then looked out the windows to the foggy abyss beyond, his brows up.

Emma followed his gaze, smiling slightly at Alfred's reaction to his brother's behavior. She found it very odd herself—one needn't even step out of doors to get a taste of just how cold the temperatures were. The draft coming in through some of the windows and down the chimneys was chilling. She had also heard Lady Dayton speaking to the housekeeper about delaying the washing of linens, as there wasn't enough access to unfrozen water.

If Lieutenant Warrilow had left the house on Emma's account— to spare her interaction with him—she would feel awful. Particularly if he were to come to any harm while away.

If only she had left London a day earlier or perhaps insisted that her father himself take the engagement gift to Alfred and Miss Bolton after the holidays.

But it was hardly useful to dwell on *what ifs*. She was at Norfield, and she had agreed to act toward the lieutenant with as much good- will as she could muster.

EMMA STARED at a blank spot on the painted wall, standing still as her maid did the last fastenings on her evening dress.

Dinner wasn't for another two hours, but Lady Dayton had kindly asked if Emma wanted to assist with the Christmas decora- tions, to which Emma had responded heartily in the affirmative. They could begin the decorations, sit down for dinner, and then continue decorating in the drawing room while they awaited the men.

Lieutenant Warrilow still hadn't returned from his expedition out of doors, a fact which worried Emma more than she cared to admit.

The maid's voice broke in on her thoughts. "I brought some of the clippings of the boughs from below stairs, Miss. I was wondering if you would like me to put some in your hair perhaps?"

Emma smiled and assented. She could always trust her maid to make her hair look precise.

The room smelled of pine, and, with the fire in the grate, she felt a pang of sadness. Christmas Eve wouldn't be the same this year, missing out on decorating her own home with her family. The Warrilows certainly wouldn't celebrate on the same scale Emma was accustomed to, but knowing she would be able to help with whatever decorations they *did* have was comforting. There was something enchanting about the smells and feelings of the Christmas season.

Joan stuck a last pin in Emma's hair, asked if she needed anything else, and then left the room. Emma lingered in front of the mirror for a moment, tweaking one of the pine clippings which protruded from the simple knot in her hair.

She stared at her reflection critically, consciously smoothing out her furrowed brow. Lieutenant Warrilow had doubted her ability to treat him kindly, and for some reason, it had grated her to hear him say it. He had said it as if it were a conscious choice she was making rather than the natural, inevitable result of his deplorable conduct toward Lucy.

And then he had smiled down at her, and she had found herself smiling back—not a forced smile as part of the truce they were making, but one of shared amusement.

It had confused her, the thread of kinship linking them in that brief moment, even as her conscience convicted her of disloyalty to Lucy and volatility in her sentiments.

She would have to make an effort to look at him with Lucy's

charity rather than the rancor that had characterized her feelings toward him for so long.

A large gusty chill enveloped her at the base of the stairs, making the hairs stand up in the small patch of bare skin between her gloves and her sleeves. The sounds of a commotion in the entry hall met her ears, and she went toward it, her curiosity winning against the desire to make her way as quickly as possible to the nearest fire.

"If we can get it through this doorway, I think we shall have no problem afterward. It was unwise to pass it through with the top first." The voice of Lieutenant Warrilow carried through the entrance hall, drifting in on the icy breeze. His voice was husky, as if under exertion.

Overcome with interest, Emma peeked through the doorway to the entry hall.

The front door was open, letting in a glacial draught which slipped around a man whose face was covered by a large scarf. He held the bottom end of a snow-dusted tree, while Lieutenant Warrilow held the top end with his uninjured arm. They took two more steps in, and the man at the tree base lowered his end, reaching to close the front door behind him. Lieutenant Warrilow removed one of his supporting hands, rotating his shoulder.

Mouth open and eyes wide and blinking, Emma stared, backing up a pace.

Lieutenant Warrilow turned at the sound. His nose and eyes were red, and he met Emma's gaze with an unreadable expression that seemed to carry some hesitation.

"What are you doing?" Emma blinked twice and looked down, realizing how uncivil her words sounded. "I am sorry," she said, shaking her head in embarrassment. "I only meant to ask: is this what you have been doing all day?" Surely there was another reason for the tree than the one that first came to mind.

Lieutenant Warrilow chuckled lightly, turning away to pull the tree farther into the entrance hall. "Yes. It is what I believe your family would call a *Christbaum*." He looked at it with a critical eye.

"Though I admit it is in a sad state. The heavy snowfall has made all the pines and firs on the property droop pitifully."

Emma's eyes slowly traveled to the tree without actually seeing it. "I think we are the only family in the county who follows such a tradition."

Lieutenant Warrilow set the top of the tree onto the floor below, removing his hat with a heavily-gloved hand and stepping toward Emma.

His brows furrowed, and his lips pressed together. "I didn't want you to have to forgo anything simply because you are forced to spend Christmas away from your family."

Emma felt her eyes sting, and she blinked furiously, swallowing to suppress the emotion welling up.

Lieutenant Warrilow watched her, and his hand moved toward hers before dropping to his side. "I have upset you," he said softly.

Emma shook her head, staring at the tree and the servant who stood next to it, chafing his hands and pointedly avoiding her gaze. "No," she said. "Of course not. I simply don't know what to say." She looked up at the lieutenant, noting how his eyes gazed down at her in concern.

Whenever she had thought about him since he'd left to war, she had imagined him with cold, calculating eyes, not the warm and attentive ones that looked down at her now. Her imagination must have rewritten her memory to conform to her opinion of him. Had he changed? Or was her opinion wrong all along?

She shivered and wrapped her arms around herself as a chill ran down her spine. "What were you thinking, going outside when the world is frozen over? Particularly after you prohibited *me* from leaving the house." She raised one brow.

His face relaxed, and he laughed, loosening the scarf which was wrapped around his neck. "I didn't prohibit you," he said. "I merely *requested* that you not attempt a journey in this weather. But if you must know, I was thinking partly of my own sanity. I can't abide being cooped up inside for too long. One of the effects of sleeping in a tent for three years, I suppose."

Emma smiled, still feeling bewildered. Her inclination was to express gratitude toward him. He had gone significantly out of his way to cater to her feelings. But how was she to square this behavior with what she had come to believe of him? This gesture was far and above what she'd had in mind when she suggested a truce.

And why did she find it so hard to simply thank him? She couldn't remember when anyone had done something so thoughtful for her—or at such a cost—and yet, her pride flared up whenever she tried to form words to express her thanks.

What had she become that she couldn't do such a simple, civil thing? Hadn't she been the one to suggest that they put aside their differences for the time being?

She looked up at him, at the brown eyes that watched her with none of the malice that she had harbored toward him for so long. She thought of her flippant comments to Lucy about him not coming home from the war—this man who had just ventured into the frigid cold to cut down a Christmas tree so that she would feel more at home.

"Thank you," she said in a soft voice, her hands placed over her stomach, as though she needed to keep in the mess of thoughts and emotions swirling around inside her.

He nodded gently. "It was my pleasure."

Emma felt out of her depth, deprived of the resentment which had for so long given her a sense of direction and grounding. She felt rudderless without it as she faced the lieutenant and his unaccountable kindness.

"I should be helping your mother to decorate," she said suddenly, glancing down the corridor behind her toward the drawing room. "Thank you again, lieutenant." She turned on her heel and walked with quick steps, anxious to put distance between herself and Lieutenant Warrilow.

She had prepared herself to set aside her feelings about the lieutenant's past actions, to look past them for a few days. In her mind, the truce had been an act of shifting her feelings from full view to a safe but temporary hiding place behind her, much like a magician might do, only to take them up again, unchanged, once she knew she would not be tainting the otherwise-joyful reunion of the Warrilows.

She had *not* anticipated that those feelings would begin to crumble through her fingers, leaving her hands grasping for the familiar but now-elusive shape she had come to know through years of handling it and inspecting it.

She pushed open the drawing room door, feeling a gush of warmth on her skin and the scent of pine meet her nose. A fire crackled in the grate, and Lady Dayton sat in front of a table covered in garlands and fruit and boughs.

She looked up at Emma's entrance and her mouth stretched into a large smile. "Ah, there you are. Come help me with this, my dear. I can't seem to make these branches cooperate."

Emma walked over to where Lady Dayton was surrounded by the makings of a kissing bough, the tabletop littered with needles from the evergreen clippings and holly, which she was trying to arrange into an orb.

Emma took the branches from her, working deftly to interweave the prickly holly branches with their bright red berries into the sphere of pine.

Lady Dayton looked on in admiration. "Thank heaven I had Mrs. Howell get all of this in town a few days ago, or else we should have nothing at all to decorate with. Don't worry, though," she said with a mischievous grin. "I took care that it shouldn't be stored in the house —the last thing I wish is to bring bad luck upon us. It took three of the servants to push the kitchen door open so that Mrs. Howell could bring it inside this morning."

The drawing room door opened, and Lieutenant Warrilow stepped halfway into the room. His mouth broke into a wide smile upon seeing his mother. "Mama," he said, his voice still slightly breathless.

She stood up, two pears rolling onto the floor from her lap. "There you are! And safe!"

"Of course I am," he said with a teasing grin. "I left you under strict orders not to worry yourself over me." He looked around the room. "Where would you like us to put it?"

Lady Dayton followed his gaze around the room. "Put what, my dear?"

He disappeared for a moment only to reappear, hoisting a large fir tree so that it stood straight, a full head taller than he. "This," he said. "Your *Christbaum*."

Lady Dayton's eyes widened, unblinking. "Good gracious! Is this what you were doing?"

Hugh smiled and nodded, hoisting the tree farther into the room where he set it against the wall and rested for a moment, his breath coming quickly and a slight crease in his brow as he pressed on his shoulder.

"But..." Lady Dayton said, fumbling over her words, "whatever for?"

Emma felt that it was time to step in and explain. "It is my fault, my lady. My mother has always insisted that we follow her family's German traditions for *Weihnachten*. This"— she nodded toward the tree —"is one of those traditions."

Lady Dayton's eyes shifted to her son, resting on him with warmth and understanding. "Ah, of course."

Lady Dayton eagerly entered into the spirit of the *Christbaum*, asking Emma what was to be done with it and how it was to be decorated. She seemed particularly pleased upon discovering that it was to be lit with candles.

Soon enough, Alfred and Miss Bolton arrived on the scene, and having had the presence of the large tree explained to them, the group began decorating the tree and the room together. Spirits were high as the lieutenant and Alfred tried to rally the group in singing long-since forgotten carols and as Emma instructed the group on how to decorate a *Christbaum* properly, channeling Oma's precision and opinionated guidance from years ago.

Emma hardly regarded the little twinge of sadness she felt at being absent from her own family's festivities.

She offered to take a small wreath of holly and ivy to the front door, where she shivered as she hung it, glancing at the snow which glittered in the moonlight. Upon her return, the sounds of merriment coming from within the drawing room greeted her, and she paused on the threshold to admire the scene.

Miss Bolton and Alfred were working together, their heads close, as they placed boughs of evergreen above the fireplace, interspersed with candles and apples. Lady Dayton was laughing, a hand covering her mouth, as Lieutenant Warrilow draped a garland around her shoulders—one that matched the wreath he had placed on his own head like a crown. He twirled her around, and they laughed as the wreath fell down over his eyes.

Was this the man Lucy had fallen in love with? The one who went out of his way to make Emma feel comfortable? Who made his mother laugh and dance? The one whose grave countenance broke into a smile until he was hardly recognizable?

But then where was the man who had left Lucy heartbroken and alone? The one who had done it without regard for the shame she would face—the whispers and stares; the pity? The one who had the audacity to ask Emma for a dance after jilting her sister?

Surely that man was there somewhere, but Emma was finding it harder and harder to recognize any vestige of such a person in the lieutenant she was coming to know.

❧ 6 ❧

Hugh stepped into the breakfast room on Christmas morning with a skipping heartbeat. A night of decorating with his family and Emma had given him more hope than he dared allow himself. He hadn't thought it possible to see Emma smile in his presence, much less smile at *him*. But she had.

And yet there had also been moments of disappointment—moments where he saw a trace of anger rekindled in Emma's eyes. She never treated him uncivilly—apparently, she took her part in the truce seriously—but he had recognized easily enough whenever the shift in her mood had occurred, when her good humor had taken on a more forced quality.

His mother had seemed not to notice, though. She had looked to be in a state of blissful contentment, having her two sons with her for the first time in years.

She had taken to the idea of the tree with great vivacity, and Hugh had watched her with enjoyment as she presented decoration ideas to Emma, who laughed appreciatively and explained what ones were most commonly seen on the *Christbaums* of her youth, when her grandmother had been alive to direct the affair properly.

Hugh had caught himself more than once, holding a decoration suspended as he watched Emma take each folded paper flower from Miss Bolton and place them carefully between the boughs of the tree. Her cheeks were becomingly flushed, and her light brown hair glinted in the light of the fire and candles, reminding Hugh of the gold ornamentation he had seen in many of the Spanish cathedrals he had seen while on campaign.

As he had watched Emma patiently teach Miss Bolton how to cut and fold paper into the likeness of a rose, he had felt eyes on him. Alfred's gaze was trained on him with an evaluative expression, but he turned away after catching eyes with Hugh.

Hugh's neck had infused with warmth, and he had adjusted one of the candles in the window frame incrementally, avoiding his brother's gaze. Had Alfred seen through Hugh—guessed at the state of his heart?

No one but Hugh knew the precise reasons behind his refusal to marry Lucy. It had been inconceivable to most—abandoning a long-expected match between the two oldest in families with neighboring lands, both of genteel means and amiable dispositions.

When asked by his father to account for his inexcusable behavior, Hugh had only apologized and maintained his position obstinately.

He had second-guessed himself a hundred times since then, regretting the heartache he had caused. He hadn't realized just how intense Lucy's feelings had been, and he hated to be the cause of her agony—strange as it was to think he could evoke such emotion within someone. If she had truly known him, she would not have felt such strong attachment to him.

But time and time again, he ended in asking himself the same question. What was more honorable: meeting the expectations of society by marrying someone in name while his heart belonged to her sister? Or causing misery and heartache for a time while ultimately freeing her from a future of pain and disappointment with a man she had wrongly exalted, one who would be fighting against his heart's wishes in secret?

Besides his father, Hugh was the last one to the breakfast table, and the conversation was focused on the expected events of the day. The cold had not abated, nor had the fog lifted. Where the day would normally be spent receiving tokens of appreciation from their tenant families, there was little likelihood of it this year, given the weather.

"I can only imagine," said Emma, "how the villagers must be faring in this frigid weather." She shuddered lightly, her hands cupped around her hot tea.

Hugh looked at her thoughtfully as he sat down and placed his napkin on his lap. He had been so caught up in the situation with Emma and in Alfred's predicament that he hadn't even thought of the effect of weather on the tenants. It seemed selfish and silly now; irresponsible, even.

"I know of one house," he said, "that is particularly ill-equipped to guard against cold like this. Unless improvements have been made since I was here last?" He looked to Alfred who shook his head.

"We were planning various adjustments and renovations for the spring."

Hugh grimaced. "We must hope that this cold is short-lived."

"Is there not something we could do," Emma said, slight hesitation in her voice, "to ensure their well-being, if only temporarily?"

Hugh and the others looked to her, and her eyes flitted around to each of theirs. "The necessary repairs might be impossible for the time being," she reasoned, "but might we not provide other means of protection against this unbearable chill?"

Of course. It was an idea that *should* have occurred to him. If he was to inherit Norfield, he would have to think of such things.

"What a wonderful idea, my dear," said Lady Dayton. "Perhaps we can gather any spare clothing and linens."

"Yes," Alfred chimed in, "but how shall we ever transport it? The roads are as icy as I've ever seen them, besides this thick fog. I shouldn't care to drive ten feet in such conditions!"

Hugh pursed his lips for a moment then looked to his mother, a small smile forming on his face. "Do we still have the sleds?" He glanced at Alfred, confident that his brother would appreciate the reference.

The corner of Alfred's mouth pulled up in a half-smile, and he narrowed his eyes. "I saw them a few weeks ago in the stables. Why?"

Hugh wagged his eyebrows. "We can transport everything ourselves using the sleds, of course."

Alfred's fork hung in the air on the way to his mouth. "In that?" He indicated the windows with his raised brows.

Hugh shrugged, pouring milk into his tea. "If you're afraid of a little chill, then you might stay here, I suppose." He looked up at Alfred with a mischievous smile trembling on his lips.

Alfred narrowed his eyes in response. "Of course I'm not afraid of the cold."

Lady Dayton interjected. "It is a very kind thought, Hugh. But Alfred is right to hesitate. Unless you bundle up sufficiently, it will be dangerous. Besides, what of your arm?" She glanced at his shoulder.

Hugh nodded, swallowing his tea. "I learned well how to keep out the cold during my winters on campaign, Mama. And I have also learned how to make do with one good shoulder. You needn't worry."

Miss Bolton reached her hand over to Alfred's, grasping it. "You shan't stay out long, shall you?"

How in the world could Alfred worry about Miss Bolton wishing to be released from their engagement when she looked at him like that? He was a fool.

What Hugh wouldn't give to see the same caring and concern in Emma's eyes.

"Well," the prosaic voice of Emma broke in on the conversation, "*I* don't see why the men should have all the adventure. What do you say we join them, Miss Bolton?"

Hugh's head came up from spreading preserves on his toast, and Emma sent him an impish, challenging look before looking back to Miss Bolton for a response.

Miss Bolton sputtered slightly, and Alfred intervened, shaking his head. "There is no need to subject yourself to such discomfort. And frankly, there is no need for us to do it, either." He looked to Hugh. "It's something the servants could do, surely."

Hugh shrugged. "If you prefer to leave the fun to them, certainly. But I think it would mean much more to the tenants coming from us, besides being much more of an adventure, as Miss Caldwell pointed out."

Alfred pursed his lips. "Fine," he said, turning to Miss Bolton. "But there is no obligation at all for you, Alice."

Miss Bolton's eyes traveled to the windows and then to the fireplace which housed a fading fire. Her jaw seemed to set, and she smiled at Alfred. "It is only for a short time, though, isn't it? And I should very much like to spend the day with you."

With such a flattering reason provided, Hugh was unsurprised to see Alfred's eyes warm as he returned Miss Bolton's suddenly shy regard.

Hugh didn't know whether to feel anticipation or apprehension, though, at the thought of carrying out their plan in the company of Emma. He was glad for an opportunity to spend more time with her, but he knew he shouldn't be.

The next two hours were spent gathering supplies from around the house to take to the villagers. Firewood was loaded onto the sleds as a base, then covered with baskets of loaves of bread, fruit, and preserves with carefully rolled spare coats, hats, and blankets surrounding. Emma offered suggestions of other items that might be of use and then took it upon herself to beautify the baskets, tying ribbons around the handles and then writing cards with sprigs of holly inside to place with the baskets.

Hugh and the three others parted ways to change into their warmest attire—of which Miss Bolton's and Emma's was supplemented by the Warrilows—meeting in the entrance hall twenty minutes later, where the servants had transported the baskets.

Hugh smiled upon seeing the others bundled up with wool scarves and mittens, extra coats and hats. Emma looked adorably plump, with only a fraction of her face visible above the scarf and below the hat she wore.

"I would suggest that we stay in the warmth as long as possible," he said, "but the truth is that we would all begin to sweat, and then we should be all the colder when we did venture outside. So"— he motioned to the door which a servant moved to open —"let us brave the wilderness without further delay."

The door opened, and Hugh breathed in, feeling the cold air as it moved down his throat and into his lungs. Miss Bolton gasped slightly, and Alfred asked whether she hadn't perhaps changed her mind.

"For I shouldn't blame you in the least," he said. "Hugh always has the most preposterous ideas."

Assured by Miss Bolton that she had no intention of staying indoors while the others went out and about, Alfred nodded with a grimace and began assisting with the loading of baskets onto the two wooden sleds. Both sleds had a seat inside, big enough for two small children, giving them the appearance of miniature sleighs. One was carved in the design of a horse, while the second was slightly smaller and plainer.

"Naturally, that one was Hugh's," Alfred said, laughing and pointing to the one carved like a horse. "He was never content with anything but the best."

Hugh glanced at Emma, who smiled perfunctorily at Alfred's comment and then turned to pick up a basket. Hugh had no difficulty in guessing what Alfred's comment had brought to her mind: that Lucy hadn't been considered "the best."

He let out a small sigh. She would never understand him, and there would always be someone's offhand comment to bring Hugh's faults to the forefront of her mind.

With the baskets loaded onto the sleds, the servants returned to the house, blowing into their hands to warm them, while Hugh, Alfred, Miss Bolton, and Emma turned to the path ahead: an untrodden expanse of snow, bathed in fog.

The servants had attached rope to the sleds, winding it around the front of the runners so that Hugh and Alfred could pull the loaded sleds without too much effort, though Hugh was obliged to use his weaker, uninjured arm. The snow crunched under their feet and sparkled slightly in the diffuse light of the cloudy day.

"Miss Bolton and I are placing our well-being in your hands, you know," Emma said in a playful voice as she glanced at Hugh and Alfred. "For I haven't the slightest idea in which direction the village lies and shouldn't know up from down if it weren't for gravity holding me to the ground. Everything looks the same under this snow."

Hugh smiled back at her. "Be at ease. Happily for you, Alfred and I could both traverse this path blindfolded."

Alfred and Miss Bolton naturally gravitated together, leaving Hugh and Emma to walk side by side. With the dense fog, even the short distance between the two pairs made for a hazy view of Alfred and Miss Bolton.

Hugh saw Emma rearrange her bonnet and the cap underneath out of the corner of his eye, covering her ears for a moment with her gloves.

"Regretting your decision already, Miss Caldwell?" said Hugh, tugging the sled over a mound of snow which had dropped from the tall oak branches above.

"Not a bit of it!" she said, marching with added vigor. "I have always wished for a snowy Christmas, and I intend to take full advantage now that my wish has been granted."

"Surely the enjoyment lies in the picturesque view the snow creates rather than in firsthand experience with it?"

"What preposterous ideas you have, Mr. Warri"— she paused and inclined her head —"*Lieutenant* Warrilow. Lucy would chastise me if she heard me refer to you without your rank."

Hugh's brows flicked upward. "She would?" So, Lucy didn't despise him, after all.

Emma nodded and brushed a patch of snow off her redingote. "Decidedly she would. Does that surprise you?"

Hugh nodded slowly. "I had been wondering if she hated me. And not without reason." He said the last words in a low voice, more to himself than to Emma.

"Well," Emma said matter-of-factly, "you are quite wrong. She won't hear a word against you and is forever reminding me of all your laudable traits."

Hugh frowned. What laudable traits did she attribute to him? "I rather thought she would never forgive me," Hugh said, his eyes staring ahead, unfocused.

"She forgave you almost instantly, I believe," Emma said, her voice softer than before. "Lucy couldn't hold a grudge if she tried. You shouldn't confuse my behavior for hers. She is a much better person than I."

Her expression was grave and thoughtful, her gaze trained on the tracks of the sled ahead of them. The only sound was the sliding of the runners on the hard snow and the crunching of their feet with each step.

"I don't fault you, you know," he said gently. "Your hostility toward me is evidence of your love and concern for your sister."

She swallowed and looked at him, as if trying to see whether he was in earnest. "I wish I could forgive the way she does, but..." she trailed off, biting her lip. "I think she might let you hurt her all over again if given the chance, you know."

Hugh blew a puff of air through his nose, and the warm cloud it created expanded in front of him. "I never wished to hurt her. I did what I thought would cause the least amount of pain."

"The least amount of pain?" Emma said incredulously. She scoffed lightly and looked at him with a measuring gaze, the same upward tilt to her chin which he had seen so often since his return home. It was obstinacy. "Why did you do it?"

He grimaced. How could he possibly explain it to her satisfaction without betraying his feelings for her? Perhaps he could have done so if those feelings were simply a distant memory—a youthful fancy he had outgrown.

But the truth was that he still loved her. More than ever, perhaps. He loved her despite how much she despised him.

He exhaled, producing another cloud of fog even thicker than what already surrounded them. "I don't think that my answer would be satisfactory to you. I can only say that it was not purely selfish. There certainly was a selfish element to it, but it was more than that. Unbelievable as it sounds to you, it was for her as much as for any other reason."

He chanced a glance at her and was surprised to discover that she was still watching him, as if she didn't know what to make of him. Surely that was an improvement from the unalloyed ire she had felt toward him for the last three years.

But it was what she had promised—to treat him with civility, to stifle her true feelings.

Temporarily.

She slipped on a hard patch of snow, and Hugh reached out to steady her with his free arm, ignoring the way the quick reaction made his shoulder sting.

She thanked him with only a hint of reluctance, her gaze flitting to his hand still holding onto her arm.

He dropped it immediately, and she let out a sigh.

"Whatever it was that led you to behave in such a way, I can only say that you can have no notion of the pain that followed. If *my* behavior is evidence of how much I care for Lucy, *her* suffering was evidence of how much she cared for you. I am certain no man could wish for anything more than to be loved as well as Lucy loved you."

He closed his eyes and swallowed. "Your sister is the best and kindest of women. I have never doubted that. But the truth is that she loved a caricature of me—a man who didn't exist in the form she believed in." He looked ahead with a blank stare. "She would have spent the remainder of her life disappointed by reality."

Emma glanced at him, and her grave expression lingered for a moment before it morphed into a half-smile. "Well, of course, *I* shan't pretend that I think Lucy's admiration for you at all merited."

She sent him a teasing smile, and he couldn't resist smiling in return. "Yes, whatever your sister believes me to be, surely no one stands in any doubt that you hold a view quite opposite of Lucy's when it comes to me. Indeed, your opinion of me couldn't be more generally understood than if you had shouted it from the housetops."

Her faced twisted into an expression part-outrage, part-laughter. Picking up a handful of snow, she threw it at him.

He put up his arm to block it, feeling the way his shoulder creaked.

"You are insufferable," she said without hostility.

His eyebrows went up as he suppressed a smile. "It is true, is it not?"

Her chin came up, but then she laughed softly. "Perhaps I was overzealous in my reaction."

His arm brushed against hers, and he noted the almost-imperceptible shift she made to create enough distance between them that it wouldn't happen again.

His smile faded, and he widened the gap between them even more. Emma would have to be the one to close any distance between them. An attempt by him to do so would be distasteful to her.

She wished for the distance, and he would not force proximity upon her. But he couldn't help hoping that perhaps her hatred toward him was melting.

7

By the time the four of them arrived in the village, Emma could barely feel her toes. The snowy landscape had been as visually enchanting as she had ever hoped it would be, with a thick sheet of pure white fluff covering every surface within eyesight. The fog had only added to the mystique of the scene, and Emma wished that Lucy could have enjoyed it with her.

What would Lucy think to know that Emma was, at this very moment, walking side-by-side with the man whose name she had hardly been able to bear uttering for so long?

Ironically, in the frigid harshness of the winter landscape, Emma had found herself thawing slightly toward Lieutenant Warrilow. Emma disliked the realization of what was transpiring within her.

When Lieutenant Warrilow had teased her for the infamy of her opinion of him, it had given her pause. It was true that anyone who knew both Emma and the lieutenant could hardly be unaware of her enmity toward him.

Emma again found herself confronting the fact that her opinion stood out in its harshness. Even those who had initially decried his behavior as shameful or cowardly had since forgiven him. Lieutenant

69

Warrilow was still well-liked whenever he came up in conversation. People would lament what he had done, but they would invariably counter Emma's harsh judgments with some qualifying compliment.

The lieutenant's claim that Lucy had put him on a pedestal—a claim with which Emma was in full agreement—reverberated in her head and heart. Emma certainly didn't put him on a pedestal. Far from it!

Had she perhaps done the opposite to him? Had she painted him, as Lucy had implied, with too broad a brush?

If Lucy's forgiveness of the lieutenant spoke to Lucy's character rather than to Lieutenant Warrilow's, surely it would follow that Emma's own stubborn grudge said more about her than it did about the lieutenant?

How could she never have considered that? She cringed to consider what it said about her.

She looked over at Lieutenant Warrilow. He was pulling the sled behind him, rotating his injured shoulder with a tense jaw.

She knew almost nothing about him since he had left to war. How had he been injured? Where had it happened? What was it like to fight in a war?

He must have felt her eyes on him, since he looked over at her. The wrinkled brow and grimace disappeared, and he smiled politely at her.

She turned her head away, suddenly unsure how to act around him.

The four of them pulled their sleds from door to door, greeting the villagers and handing each family a basket. Emma had expected to find herself wishing for an invitation into the warm homes, for a recess from the bitter cold outside.

But there were no roaring fires within the homes they visited. Shivering children with red noses came to stand by their mothers at the door. They seemed to be wearing every scrap of clothing they owned to keep out the cold. One mother burst into tears at the sight of their offering.

They left her door, each of them silent as the bittersweet weight of the woman's gratitude rested on their minds and shoulders. Emma watched Lieutenant Warrilow shake his head, his brow deeply furrowed. "Some of them are much worse off than I thought. They need more than we have brought. We must send more supplies tomorrow."

Emma nodded her agreement. "I had the same thought."

With only two houses left, Alfred glanced at his pocket watch. "It is getting late, Hugh. Perhaps we can divide and conquer for these last two. We can take this house." He indicated the house to their right with a tip of his scarf-swathed head.

"No," Hugh replied. "If you don't mind, I should like to make the visit to that house. An old friend lives there."

"Oh, right," Alfred nodded. "Mr. Banks. Go ahead, then." He pulled the sled behind him, with only one basket remaining inside, as Miss Bolton walked alongside him.

Emma followed Lieutenant Warrilow to the chipped and faded wooden door. Unlike some of the other houses, there was no evidence of footsteps in the snow outside the door. It lay undisturbed.

The lieutenant rapped on the door three times.

They waited patiently, but all seemed silent, save for the creak of a door opening for Alfred and Miss Bolton behind them, across the road.

She looked at the lieutenant, but he was staring at the door, unperturbed by the lack of response.

A muffled thudding emanated from the house, growing louder as it approached, and soon enough the door opened, revealing a short, bearded man with a balding head and a wooden leg. He looked at Emma first and then to Lieutenant Warrilow. Recognition lit up his eyes.

"Lieutenant," he said, saluting him even as his eyes welled with tears.

"Banks," Lieutenant Warrilow said in a gruff voice, closing the distance between them and embracing the man heartily.

Emma blinked, wondering what she was witnessing.

"Well," said Banks in a jovial voice, "don't stand out there! Come in!"

With a quick glance behind him at his brother, Lieutenant Warrilow smiled and accepted, allowing Emma to pass in front of him.

Though still nowhere near the temperatures Emma was accustomed to indoors, the house was decidedly warmer than outside, and she felt her frozen nose begin to thaw and then run.

Lieutenant Warrilow, too, was sniffling sporadically, but Emma couldn't be sure how much of it was due to the change in temperature and how much was the result of whatever emotion the sight of Mr. Banks had elicited. He introduced Emma to Mr. Banks who expressed his pleasure at the honor of making her acquaintance and then invited them to sit down on the only two chairs in the room.

Emma thanked him and took a seat, but Lieutenant Warrilow insisted that Mr. Banks occupy the other chair, maintaining that he would be comfortable enough on the wood floor.

"Injured in the war?" Mr. Banks asked, indicating the lieutenant's arm.

Lieutenant Warrilow nodded. "At Vitoria," he said as he lowered himself to sit against the wall near the fire, stretching one leg out and bending the other.

"Is it healing?" Banks asked.

Lieutenant Warrilow tipped his head from side to side and shrugged. "Well enough, though it dislikes this cold."

"Can you blame it?" Mr. Banks said with a chuckle. He looked at Emma. "This man saved my life, you know." He nodded toward Lieutenant Warrilow who shook his head.

"It's true, admit it or no," Mr. Banks continued. "I'd have lost much more than this leg if not for you."

"You're becoming a bit of a bore, Banks," said Lieutenant Warrilow, draping his arm over his knee. "Tell me, though, how have you fared since your return?"

Mr. Banks shifted in his seat, and his wooden leg thumped on the floor as he moved it. "Better than I could have hoped, thanks to you." He turned toward Emma. "You've found the finest gentleman in all of England, Miss."

Emma felt heat flood her cheeks and stuttered, but Lieutenant Warrilow intervened, saying with a wry smile, "You're off the mark, Banks. And if she weren't so polite, Miss Caldwell would heartily disagree with you."

Mr. Banks's head drew back as he looked at Emma. "What do you mean?"

She shot Lieutenant Warrilow a fulminating glance, but his eyes sparkled back at her, full of humor.

Mr. Banks let out a "hmph" and scooted his chair closer to Emma's. "Let me tell you something about that man there."

Lieutenant Warrilow made an impatient gesture with his hand. "Have done, Banks."

Mr. Banks ignored him, and he leaned forward, resting his elbows on his knees. "It's a good man that saves another man's life once; but what do you say of a man who saves the same man's life twice?"

Lieutenant Warrilow pushed himself up off the floor with a scoffing noise. "If this is your idea of pleasant conversation, Banks, I can tell you that it is not mine." He shrugged his great coat back on and wrapped his scarf around his neck. "I must go tell my brother and Miss Bolton to join us here, as I'm sure they're wondering what has happened to us." He looked at Emma with one eyebrow raised. "You mustn't pay any heed to what Banks says, Miss Caldwell." He nodded and opened the front door. "I won't be but a moment."

Emma's eyes lingered on the door as it shut behind the lieutenant before she turned back to Mr. Banks. "Lieutenant Warrilow saved your life on two separate occasions?"

Mr. Banks nodded decisively. "That's right. When all the other soldiers were fleeing, he risked his life to come to my aid; carried me across the field to safety until he could find a doctor."

Emma grimaced, her eyes moving to Mr. Banks' wooden leg and then back up to his face. "And the second time?"

Mr. Banks raised a hand, indicating the room around them. "Who do you think provided me a place to come home to after I was discharged?" He cleared his throat, and Emma thought she saw his eyes take on a watery sheen. "I've no family to speak of, and losing my leg meant losing the livelihood I had before becoming a soldier." He leaned back down on his knees and gazed into the dying fire. "The good lieutenant offered me a home and work, and I've been here ever since. Almost two years now." He looked up at Emma. "Lieutenant Warrilow is the best man I know. Whatever your quarrel is with him, remember that."

Emma bit the inside of her lip and swallowed. She was finding it harder to maintain her critical opinion of Lieutenant Warrilow.

The door opened, and the lieutenant walked in, with Alfred and Miss Bolton trailing behind, kicking off the snow from their boots.

Miss Bolton was all kindness to Mr. Banks, expressing her gratitude for a chance to warm her hands, ears, and feet.

Mr. Banks moved to stand. "Please, Miss Bolton," he said, attempting to vacate the chair for her to sit in.

"Oh, no," she said, taking a step backward. "I am very comfortable standing, only I think I should like to move closer to the fire if no one minds." She smiled and moved toward the grate where only a few small flames danced on the charred logs within.

"That pitiful fire won't do, Banks," Lieutenant Warrilow said, striding over to the items they had transported from the sled. He picked up two logs and placed them into the fire, brushing his hands off after. "We will send more tomorrow. What else do you need? Only say the word."

Emma was silent, observing the lieutenant more carefully than ever before—the way he treated Mr. Banks kindly yet without condescension; how he seemed at his ease in the small, sparsely-furnished home; his ability to use humor to set others at ease.

He and Mr. Banks entertained the group with their adventures and mishaps in Spain, Mr. Banks teasing Lieutenant Warrilow for his pitiful Spanish.

"Sadly, it is all true," Hugh laughed. "More than once I found myself explaining to a local how we were in search of sustenance because we were all married. What I wished to say, of course, was that we were tired."

"*Casados* and *cansados*," Mr. Banks explained to the others, a large grin on his face.

The lieutenant shrugged. "My French, too, was always less-than-satisfactory. I wish I could say that my Spanish had improved in the two years since I last saw you, but it is every bit as atrocious as it was then."

When Emma and the others left, there were smiles on all of their faces, and Lieutenant Warrilow embraced Mr. Banks with a promise to send more supplies the next day.

With their sleds empty of their burden, the four of them began traipsing through the cold back toward Norfield Manor.

"How is it that it seems even colder than it was when we left earlier?" Emma said, hunching her shoulders and shivering.

Lieutenant Warrilow smiled down at her. "I believe it has actually warmed outside. It is the contrast of the cold so soon after sitting near the warm fire which makes it seem colder."

Emma tried to wiggle her toes inside her boots. "I gained feeling in my feet just in time to lose it again. How, precisely, does one walk without any sensation in one's toes?"

"By relying on habit, I suppose." He glanced behind him at the sled and then back to Emma, a half-smile inching up one side of his face. "But it isn't the only option available, you know."

Emma looked at the sled with misgiving mixed with curiosity. "What? And you would pull me along?"

He stopped, bowing slightly. "I am at your service, *señorita*."

Emma raised her brows. "At my service? That is a brave offer."

He narrowed his eyes in mock suspicion. "Do your worst." He

nodded toward the sled, and she stepped toward it with a provoking arch to her brows.

The sled was meant for someone much younger and smaller than Emma, and the number of layers she was wearing meant that getting in and settled was not as elegant as she had hoped it would be, somewhat undermining the calm dignity she was attempting.

Seeing her struggle, and with only the slightest trembling of his lips, Lieutenant Warrilow assisted her in and executed a flourishing bow.

Once Emma was situated, the fit was snug but comfortable enough. Certainly more comfortable than walking on frozen feet.

Lieutenant Warrilow stepped back to survey her and covered his mouth with his hand, his shoulders shaking.

"What?" Emma said, her chin up as she smoothed her skirts with great affectation.

He schooled his expression into a grave one. "Nothing at all. You look very...regal."

She looked at the sled, noting how large she seemed in the confines of the small, carved pony that would have held the lieutenant when he was a young boy. Her mouth trembled for a moment as she imagined the picture she presented.

She shifted in her seat, trying to look down her nose at the lieutenant—an awkward feat, as he was taller than her even when she stood. "I am accustomed to my sled being pulled at a clipping pace, I will have you know."

Lieutenant Warrilow's feigned great interest. "Ah, being, as you are, in the habit of traveling by sled?"

She inclined her head in a formal confirmation of his question.

"I shall make every effort not to disappoint you," he said, securing the rope in his hand and beginning to pull her cautiously forward.

Emma looked ahead where Alfred and Miss Bolton had stopped, largely concealed by the fog. They were looking back toward her and the lieutenant.

"What a capital idea," said Alfred as they approached. He took Miss Bolton's hand to assist her into the sled.

"Oh," she said, allowing him to lead her with some hesitation, "are you certain it is quite safe?"

"If," Emma interjected, "he is anything like my own steed"— she indicated the lieutenant with her head —"you are much more likely to freeze to death awaiting arrival at your destination than to risk injury due to speed."

The lieutenant whipped around to face her, and Alfred threw his head back. "A blow to your pride, Hugh. And a challenge perhaps? I am determined that Alice shall find nothing to complain of in *her* transportation."

Lieutenant Warrilow's eyes held Emma's, and she pursed her lips to keep from smiling. "If it is speed you wish for," he said, "then speed you shall have."

Alfred rubbed his hands together in delight. "A race, then!" He ensured that Miss Bolton was safely deposited in the sled, then put one foot in front of the other, readying himself for a quick start.

The lieutenant seemed to enter into the spirit of things, pulling his gloves on more snugly and tugging the tops of his boots upward before setting his feet in order.

"Now, Alfred," he said, "mind you I haven't the advantage of pulling with my strong arm."

Alfred chuckled. "Making excuses for losing already, Hugh?"

The lieutenant scoffed and grabbed for the rope with his uninjured arm. He looked to his brother with an exaggerated challenge in his eyes and called, "Ready, steady, *go!*"

The sleds jerked forward, and Emma exclaimed in surprise, gripping the sides and feeling thankful that the fullness of her clothing prevented her from flying from her seat as she otherwise might have.

The cold air whipped at her bonnet and scarf, making her eyes sting; puffs of snow landed on her face and clothing, kicked up from the careless steps of the lieutenant and Alfred. Her mouth stretched into a wide grin, a laugh full of relish and surprise escaping her.

Miss Bolton seemed to be in a state of half-terror, half-delight, her eyes wide and alert, and her mouth displaying teeth in turns clenching and smiling.

The Warrilow brothers were all concentration as their boots poked holes into the snow below with the force of their running. Lieutenant Warrilow looked back toward Emma, his full smile on display as he called to her in a breathless shout, "Is this more to your taste, Miss Caldwell?"

With his eyes on Emma instead of the terrain in front of him, he veered closer to the other sled, misstepped, and collided with Alfred. They collapsed in a hectic tangle, puffs of snow springing into the air, while the position they landed in caused the ropes to pull awkwardly at the sleds, tipping Emma's onto its side.

She cried out, still laughing, as she toppled over with the sled, completely at the mercy of forces beyond her control, sliding into the snow.

Alfred was laughing breathlessly, and Emma heard the sound of crunching of snow nearing as her laughs died out. The lieutenant was crawling toward her with an anxious expression.

"Miss Caldwell," he said between breaths. "Are you hurt?"

She offered no response, trying to catch her breath from laughing as she turned to lie on her back, spreading her arms to each side as her cheeks ached from smiling. She looked upward at the foggy skies above, feeling completely enveloped in a world of white.

Lieutenant Warrilow's face came to hover over her, obstructing her view. His knit brow relaxed upon seeing her expression, and his mouth stretched into a wide smile.

"You almost killed me," she said breathlessly, noting how his eyes were alight with the glow of the snow behind her so that she could see her own reflection in them.

"But I *didn't* kill you," he said significantly. "In fact, you seem to be in very high spirits."

She laughed, her eyes shifting to the hazy skies that surrounded him. "I feel very much alive."

"Ah," said the lieutenant, leaning back so that he could follow her gaze upward. "Sometimes it takes the prospect of death for one to appreciate life, I think." He looked at her with a teasing grin. "You are welcome."

She laughed again, grabbing a fistful of snow in her gloved hand and throwing it at him.

It was shockingly unladylike, but there was something so invigorating about the cold and the fog which gave Emma the impression that they were in another world entirely.

Lieutenant Warrilow dodged the worst of the fistful of snow, watching where it landed behind him and then turning slowly to Emma with faux-offense. "It is unwise to provoke someone whose skill is greater than yours, you know."

"Is that so?" she said, pulling another handful of snow toward her.

He raised a brow, watching her steadily as he clutched a fistful of his own, his mouth threatening a smile.

"Hey ho!" Alfred said, and Emma looked at him just in time to see him lob a snowball at Lieutenant Warrilow. To her utter surprise, Miss Bolton raised a timid arm and threw a fistful of snow toward Emma, uttering a small squeal as she did so. Only a few flecks made it to Emma's face, sprinkling her cheeks and nose with bits of cold.

"Oh dear!" Miss Bolton cried out. "I am terribly sorry."

"We are under attack, Miss Caldwell," the lieutenant said, grabbing for more snow, which he packed tightly between his two hands and then sent flying in the air.

A moment later, a snowball returned from Alfred's position, grazing Emma's arm and landing in the space between her and Lieutenant Warrilow.

"Come," the lieutenant breathed urgently, a large grin spread across his face, making him look like a young boy. He grasped her hand and pulled her up to her knees, leading her with rushed, crunching movements toward the tipped sled, which he crouched behind.

She debated whether she should protest his high-handed ways or simply embrace the fun, but a snowball whirred past her head, and she hurriedly ducked down next to him.

He let go of her hand, reaching for more snow to pack into compact balls and periodically peeking over the sled. Snowballs landed regularly in the area around them, creating pockets in the snow, and Emma began adding to the growing pile of white balls, glittering in the dispersing fog.

The assault suddenly stopped, and Emma cocked an ear, saying, "What has happened?"

She stretched her head to look over the sled, but Lieutenant Warrilow grasped her hand, pulling her down and putting a finger in front of his lips.

"It is calm before the storm," he said, leaning in to whisper. His breath grazed her face, and her heart tripped as she felt herself wanting to lean into the sweet scent rather than away from it, as she should. They were close enough that she could see that his eyelashes were darker than his brows; that they curled upward and skimmed his eyebrows when he opened his eyes fully. "We must have a strategy."

She nodded, slightly breathless.

He looked at the pile of snowballs, packing another in his hands as he contemplated their arsenal. "I shall run out in this direction"— he pointed toward Norfield —"drawing their attack. I will run in a circle, returning once I feel confident they have used most of their stock. And then...."

"And then we attack," said Emma, unable to hide the mischief in her eyes and smile.

Lieutenant Warrilow nodded, his eyes twinkling.

She took her lips between her teeth, her breath catching as she realized how clearly she could see the grey that rimmed his irises and how the clouds their breath created mixed together.

Pretending to be on good terms with Lieutenant Warrilow was turning out to be far easier than she had imagined. Too easy.

His brows flicked up in a question, and she pulled herself together, nodding her readiness. Their eyes held for a moment, and the lieutenant popped up into a run, calling out a battle cry and leaving her with a lap full of falling snow in his wake.

She stayed low, her heart rushing in a way she decided to attribute to the thrill of the battle rather than the proximity to the lieutenant. She heard the rhythmic crunching of his boots in the snow, the soft thumping of snowballs both hitting and missing their target, the rallying cries of Alfred, and the much more timid ones of Miss Bolton.

Emma laughed softly, feeling grateful for her shelter. The sound of crunching snow grew louder while the hits became less frequent, and the lieutenant half-jumped, half-slid into position next to her, tossing snow up into her face as he came to a halt.

She stayed completely still, her skin stinging under the frozen snow. She batted her eyes to rid them of the water clinging to her lashes.

Breathing heavily and grasping at his injured shoulder, Lieutenant Warrilow shot a wary glimpse over the sled. He exhaled and slumped down, turning to Emma and saying, "I believe they have exhausted"— he stopped, scanning her face with an unsuccessful attempt to suppress a smile. "Oh dear. Have I done that?"

She nodded slowly, unblinking, keeping her expression blank. Melted snow trickled down her forehead, her cheeks, and her chin.

He bit his lip and then searched in his great coat.

She couldn't resist a smile. "Is this how you treat your allies, Lieutenant?"

He pulled out a handkerchief, wiping at the small streams of thawing snow on her face. His forehead was wrinkled in concentration, but he grinned. "No, certainly not. But we are only temporary allies, after all.

He met her eyes, and his hand slowed.

Her skin tingled, and her stomach flipped erratically. Her eyes flitted to his mouth, and she forced them back up.

Was this temporary, what she was feeling? It felt like much more than the civil terms of the truce she had suggested.

She swallowed. Surely it was simply the combination of their physical proximity, the mystical landscape, the rush of the snowball fight, and the stark contrast between her recent animosity and current friendliness toward him.

It couldn't be anything more. It simply couldn't.

"Yes," she said, turning away. "Temporary allies."

His hand stayed suspended in the air for a moment, just in front of her face, before dropping slowly.

Emma looked up. The fog was thinning, but clouds still veiled the sky above. She looked for the brightest spot in the sky, judging it to be nearing four o'clock.

"We should be getting back. I am sure your mother is fretting over our long absence by now."

Lieutenant Warrilow stood, nodding. His face was grave, the humorous twinkle no longer lighting up his eyes.

Alfred called out to them. "Surrendering, are you? Very wise choice. I'm afraid you two are no match for Alice and me!"

No, indeed. Emma and Lieutenant Warrilow were no match at all. Not a match for Alfred and Miss Bolton. And decidedly not a match for each other.

8

Hugh shrugged on his jacket of superfine blue cloth with the help of his valet.

His hands had finally stopped tingling from spending the better part of the day out of doors. The temperature seemed to be warming, though, judging from the sound of water dripping outside his window. It would all freeze overnight again, of course, but perhaps the temperatures would rise enough again the following day to melt a fair bit of what covered the landscape and roads.

That would mean the imminent departure of Emma, of course. Surely she wouldn't hesitate to leave at the earliest moment possible.

He had known that the remarkably good terms that had flourished between them all day could not last. And he had seen the very moment when Emma had realized it, too.

What had caused her to look at him with such dismay, he couldn't say.

Nor could he deny the hope he harbored: that she had felt the same pull of attraction that he had felt. But more likely, she had simply known a moment's lapse in memory which had led her to treat him with more amiability than she had intended.

Whatever the reason, she had reverted to a distant civility toward him, politely refusing his offer to take her up in the sled for the remainder of the way home and engaging Miss Bolton—sitting in the slow-moving sled pulled by Alfred—in conversation for the final ten minutes of the walk.

He had feared that the harmony between them would be short-lived, but he hadn't been able to resist responding in kind to her amiability; to teasing her, if only to see the way her dimple appeared. Seeing her look at him, free of any reserve or anger, full of enjoyment and kinship—it felt worth any cost.

But that blissful rapport was at an end. And now he was left feeling almost desperate to recapture it.

Hugh sighed and thanked his valet, dismissing him and then descending the stairs to dinner. It would be his first Christmas home in three years. Never had he imagined spending it in the company of Emma Caldwell, of all people.

Hugh's jaw came open upon seeing her, standing in the drawing room, smiling at his mother. Her white crepe dress was simple and elegant, set off with a gold-braided trim which shimmered in concert with her hair in the evening candlelight. She had never looked more angelic than in that moment.

In the company of a married couple and an engaged couple, it was only natural that Hugh would be left to walk beside Emma to the dining room. She seemed to face the prospect with equanimity as he offered her his arm, though there was a restraint in her eyes and in her manner that had been absent since their truce began.

He debated whether to match her reserve, but he couldn't refrain from an attempt to provoke a smile from her. He leaned in toward her, saying in a low voice, "And to think it was *my* grave expression which you feared would betray us."

She whipped her head around, and he smiled down at her, watching with pleasure and relief as her dimple quivered in response.

"You have played your part admirably, I admit," she said. "You are much more skilled an actor than I gave you credit for."

His expression softened. "I haven't required any skill. My part of the truce has been no act."

She looked up at him, wariness and something else in her eyes which he couldn't identify.

He would do well not to pursue that avenue of conversation.

"So," he said in a cheerful voice, looking ahead with a large intake of breath and hoping to quench the cautious light he had seen in her expression, "if we are found out, I am afraid that the blame will be entirely yours."

She scoffed. "Certainly not. If you provoke me into betraying myself, then the fault will lie with you."

He smiled, gazing back down at her. "I intend to take advantage of every opportunity to provoke you, then. For how are you to develop your acting skill if you are never challenged?"

"Perhaps you are right," she said matter-of-factly. "But so far, you have failed miserably."

He raised his brows enigmatically. "Is that a challenge? Or an admission that you have found our truce less difficult than you antici-pated? That you actually enjoy my company?"

He knew he was being bold. Too bold, likely.

They reached the doorway to the dining room, and she stopped, turning toward him to prevent their progress. "I am determined that your mother have the convivial, joyful Christmas she deserves with her prodigal son—"

Hugh opened his mouth to protest her characterization of him, but she put up her hand to silence him "—and if I must exert all my powers to *pretend*"— she shot him a significant look —"that I find pleasure in your company, so be it."

He nodded his understanding but said, "And I shall use my acting skill to pretend that I believe you."

She narrowed her eyes at him, but her mouth quivered adorably.

"You have chosen an interesting place to stop," Alfred said as he and Miss Bolton came up behind them. He indicated the top of the doorway.

Hugh and Emma both tipped their heads up, and Hugh gripped his lips together to suppress a smile.

The kissing bough hung above them, rotating ever-so-slightly.

His stomach flipped as he thought what it would be like to kiss Emma. But the kiss he imagined, the one he dreamed of would not be with an Emma who found his company distasteful—and it certainly wouldn't be in front of his brother.

So that's all it was, the vision in his mind of pressing a kiss upon those lips and having the kiss returned—it was a dream, a fool's paradise.

Hugh put up his hands in a gesture of innocence. "It was Miss Caldwell who insisted that we stop here. And"— he said, putting a finger to his lips thoughtfully —"I believe it was also Miss Caldwell who placed the bough here the other night."

Emma looked up at him with near-betrayal in her eyes. "An unhappy coincidence, I assure you!"

He shrugged. "I suppose I must believe you." He looked up at the bough again. Only a few of the berries remained. "In any case, I believe there were at least a dozen berries here when Emma strung it up, but only three have survived the day." He raised a brow and looked at Alfred. "Who in the world could be responsible for such wreckage?"

Miss Bolton flushed scarlet, and Alfred smiled down at her before looking at Hugh again, his grin wide and unabashed. "Who indeed?" He pulled Miss Bolton along with him, passing Hugh and Emma into the dining room.

Alfred's spirits were much improved since his discussion with Hugh in the library, a fact which both gladdened and unsettled Hugh. Had Alfred simply accepted that there was nothing to do but enjoy the time left with Miss Bolton? Or was he expecting Hugh to come up with a solution to the predicament?

There was not a happy end in sight for Alfred and Miss Bolton, failing some miracle. And Hugh was no closer to coming up with that miracle. If he could have given Alfred his own birthright, he thought he would even have done that. But it was not possible.

And so it was with pain that he watched Alfred and Miss Bolton's happiness together, anticipating its inevitable, unhappy ending, feeling responsible for it.

It was eerily similar to how Hugh felt about the good terms that had flourished between himself and Emma.

And he was every bit as powerless to prevent that inevitable end.

The dining table had been adorned with extra candles, a long garland of pine, which filled the room with its invigorating scent, and more of the paper flowers created by Emma and Miss Bolton.

Spirits were high, and Hugh found himself seeking out Emma each time he laughed, hoping to share with her in the delights of a holiday he knew she loved. She was in her element—and she took his breath away as she joked and sparred through the evening, her cheeks looking warm to the touch with the cheerfulness she exuded.

When they had all finished, the women stood to leave, and Hugh found himself wishing he could walk to the drawing room with Emma's slender arm wrapped in his; he found himself wishing he could ask her whether she still intended to follow through on her plan: to avoid his company once she left home after the snow melted. The prospect of not seeing her again made him feel a kind of grief and recklessness he hadn't felt since the night he had decided to enter the army. It left his chest feeling simultaneously hollow and heavy.

His return home had, so far, been nothing like he had anticipated. His priority had been to visit Seymour's family—something he had been unable to do and was unsure when he *would* be able to. If he waited until he garnered the courage, it might be never. He was much more of a coward than he had ever before realized.

And his intention to make amends with Lucy, to offer her the marriage he had denied her before? It was impossible and unnecessary.

Finally, Hugh had fallen even more deeply and hopelessly in love with the woman who was determined not to forgive him on any account. No matter that it was obvious to Hugh how utterly content they could be together, how lively their lives could be—Emma had built a wall and, much as she might give Hugh glimpses of what *could* be, she seemed to have no intention of deconstructing the wall.

Alfred stood, a glass of port in hand, and walked over to the window. Looking past the curtain into the dark vista beyond the window, he said, "I don't know whether to be glad or upset that the temperature seems to be rising and the snow beginning to melt, but it is decidedly warmer this evening than it was last night." He stared out of the window a moment longer and then shut the curtain with more force than was merited, walking back to the table with a knit brow as he glanced at his father. "If it keeps up, I shall have to ride to Dunmere first thing and speak with Alice's father. I don't at all relish the prospect."

"And yet it must be done," his father said without sympathy.

Hugh swirled the crimson liquid in his glass, staring down at it and remembering the similarly-colored ring he still held in his possession. He was both anxious and unwilling to be rid of it. It was his only remaining connection to Seymour, and yet it had become a reminder of the guilt he carried for Seymour's death and the situation of his widow and children.

"Has she given you reason to believe she would like to be free of the engagement?" Hugh said.

Alfred shook his head, leaning forward so that his elbows rested on the table. "Alice has assured me that she wishes us to marry, regardless of my circumstances. She is an angel." He made a tent with his fingers, watching them as he said, "Her father, though, is much more pragmatic than Alice. He will not accept my change in fortunes so easily. I think that deep down Alice knows that he will not allow us to marry." He rubbed his forehead with a hand.

Hugh felt for Alfred. He had never coveted Hugh's position as heir, but it was natural that, once he found himself in a situation to leverage the inheritance for a chance at marriage with the woman he loved, he would be loath to part with it.

"Yes, Sir Clive is unlikely to countenance the match now," Hugh's father said baldly.

"What of your plans for the church?" Hugh said, hoping to find some way to assist Alfred. "Would he be against the match if you had prospects for a living?"

Alfred let out an explosive breath. "Don't misunderstand me, Hugh. I am terribly happy to have you home, but your timing is impeccable." He sat back and stared at Hugh. "The living at Balmaker was given to Edward Campbell not three weeks ago."

Hugh grimaced. Balmaker was the largest living for dozens of miles and one that Alfred had long wished would come vacant.

"Could you not have written, Hugh?" Alfred continued, running a hand through his hair. "To inform us that you were still alive and well? For that is the only reason that it is Campbell rather than me being installed at Balmaker. Campbell who already has the living at Holnard as well." He shook his head in frustration.

Alfred's words stung, making Hugh's pent-up frustration and guilt flare suddenly. "Surely you can't blame me for not writing when my death was clearly looked on with such jubilation."

Hugh rubbed at his mouth, already regretting the outburst.

Aghast, Alfred walked over to him and put a gentle hand on his shoulder. "You mustn't think such a thing, Hugh. You can have no notion how Mama and I"—he glanced at their father and quickly added—"and Papa have fretted over your well-being. You know I have never coveted your inheritance, surely."

Hugh nodded, only managing a grimace. Alfred's words brought him some comfort, and yet he still felt responsible for the predicament he faced.

Hugh had genuinely convinced himself for a time that his family would be better off not hearing from him, that they would ultimately be happier simply believing him to be dead or gone. The prospect of living out his life in anonymity in Spain had been terribly enticing.

It was Seymour's death which had persuaded him that he needed to return to England, to face the consequences of his conduct, no matter how people might misunderstand him and label him as a coward and a jilt. He loved his family too much to abandon them forever.

But he had never anticipated just how much havoc his decision to return would wreak—how coming home might multiply the problems he had to tackle, how impossible it would seem to face the Seymours, and how his return would change everything for Alfred.

Alfred had always been set on making a living in the church, satisfied with his prospects as a second son. And that fact crushed Hugh with guilt.

"I am sorry, Alfred," he said softly, looking up from his port.

Alfred offered no response, his expression brooding and sullen.

Hugh opened and closed his mouth. What could he possibly say? He had deprived Alfred of an inheritance and a wife in one fell swoop.

When Hugh's father stood to indicate his readiness to enter the drawing room, Hugh had to stifle his desire to jump up from his seat, so impatient was he. The mood at the dinner table was oppressive and, for whatever reason, Hugh imagined that being around Emma might relieve some of that weight.

They entered the drawing room to the sight of Emma playing the piano while Miss Bolton and Hugh's mother sang. The tune was unfamiliar to Hugh, and Emma paused periodically to remind the others of the words and tune. Likely it was a translation of one of the German Christmas songs the Caldwells had grown up singing.

Emma made a mistake in playing the keys, and Hugh's mother and Miss Bolton simultaneously confused the words of the song, making for a discordant moment. The three of them broke into laughter.

"I am woefully out of practice," Emma said, taking her hands off the keys.

"Besides accompanying a clumsy and incompetent singer," Lady Dayton said.

"Two clumsy and incompetent singers," said Miss Bolton.

"Let us simply agree," Emma said, standing and pushing the bench under the piano, "that our little trio must put out of our minds the hope of ever being invited to perform anywhere more public than this drawing room."

Hugh smiled, gratified beyond measure to see the camaraderie amongst the women—a gratification tempered by the knowledge that it was a situation unlikely to reoccur.

Once the truce between him and Emma was at an end, and if Miss Bolton and Alfred's engagement also came to an end, well, the three women in front of Hugh were unlikely to find themselves in company together again.

If Hugh only had a short time to enjoy the sociable accord, he would take full advantage of it while he could.

"Mother, Miss Caldwell, Miss Bolton," he said. "What do you say that we honor this Christmas evening by playing a game of snapdragon?"

The suggestion was received with excitement by everyone but Hugh's father, who had already installed himself in his large wing-back chair, spreading out a days-old copy of *The Morning Chronicle*, and paying no attention at all to the others in the room. Hugh's mother, on the other hand, declared that she would enjoy partici-pating as a spectator.

Alfred's expression had lightened considerably upon Hugh's suggestion, and Hugh had high hopes that, whatever the future held for the four of them, they would at least be able to enjoy themselves this one evening.

The bell was rung to request the needed components, and Hugh walked toward the nearest candle, extinguishing it with a breath. "The first step is to extinguish all of the light in the room." He smiled and walked toward the Christmas tree, alight with dozens of candles.

"Surely not the Christmas tree," Emma said, disappointed.

Hugh stopped, looking around the room at the various candles left to extinguish. "If you wish to leave these candles alight, I shan't extinguish them."

Emma smiled, staring contentedly at the tree. "There is nothing quite as magical as a dark room, illuminated by a lighted *Christbaum*."

The corner of Hugh's mouth tugged upward. Emma seemed a bit like a child when she spoke of Christmas.

When all the other candles had been extinguished, Hugh looked around the room to see the effect of the candlelit tree. The small flames reflected on the window panes, creating a mirror-effect.

Emma came up next to him, and he felt the familiar tingling her closeness provoked.

"You were right," he said, staring mesmerized at the flickering flames. "Magical is the only way to describe it."

She smiled at him, the flames reflecting in her soft eyes, and his breath hitched.

"Come," he said, forcing himself to put an end to the thoughts and emotions coursing through him, and she followed him to the table.

The four young people gathered around it, Miss Bolton and Alfred sitting next to one another on a settee while Hugh and Emma took their seats on the gray chaise lounge which Hugh had moved toward the table.

Two footmen entered, one holding a glass bowl and a bottle of brandy, the other holding a bowl of raisins and a tinderbox.

"I warn you," Emma said, "that I have never actually played this game."

"Nor I," Miss Bolton said, shifting nervously in her seat.

"Between Alfred and I, we have ample experience." He took a moment to review the rules of the game, with Alfred interjecting every now and then.

"Enough talk," Alfred said, putting down the half-full bottle of brandy and dropping a handful of raisins into the bowl. "Let us play!" He opened the tinder box, striking the steel against the flint. After four or five attempts to light the char cloth, Hugh put out his hand.

"You think you will light it more easily than I?" Alfred said skeptically.

Hugh only kept his hand out. Alfred surrendered the materials, and Hugh smiled.

With one solid strike, the char cloth ignited. "I have lit more fires over the past three years than you can possibly imagine." He lit the brandy on fire, and blue flames danced on the surface. "Ah," he said suddenly, closing the tinder box and setting it beside the bowl. He picked up a single almond from the bowl of raisins, holding it up for the others to see. "Whoever fishes *this* out of the bowl is declared the winner, no matter how many or how few raisins anyone has managed to pluck out during the game."

"And what is the benefit of such a prize?" asked Emma, removing her shawl and laying it across the end of the chaise lounge.

"The winner," Hugh said slowly, enjoying the suspense he saw in Miss Bolton and Emma's expressions, "can claim a reward of his or her choosing."

Miss Bolton looked at Alfred with flushed cheeks, and he winked at her.

Despite the initial hesitation from Miss Bolton and the skepticism of Emma, the four of them enjoyed a rousing game of snapdragon. Miss Bolton was particularly agile, and Hugh was pleasantly surprised at the way the game seemed to break through her shell of calm composure, bringing out a side of her which was lively and competitive.

Hugh's mother watched in apprehension and amusement for some time from a nearby chair, but once his father, who had been snoozing in his chair, stood and announced his intention to go to bed, she adjured them not to burn the house down and followed her husband out.

Emma was predictably competitive, determined not to let Hugh claim the almond. Little did she know that he had already done so with no fanfare, slipping it into his coat pocket with no one the wiser.

So determined was Emma, though, that she had plunged one

ungloved hand into the brandy and then made to do the same with her gloved hand, fishing inside with no regard for the blue flames which licked at her wrist.

Hugh grabbed her gloved hand by the wrist, pulling it toward him and away from the bowl and fire. The fingers were soaked with caramel-colored brandy, and small flames whipped up at the tips.

Alfred swore softly, and Miss Bolton's hand flew to her mouth.

Heart thudding in his chest, Hugh snatched a towel from the table, enveloping Emma's hand between his and pressing forcefully.

Emma cried out in pain, attempting unsuccessfully to withdraw her hand.

Hugh maintained the pressure a moment longer and then opened the towel to inspect the fingertips of the gloves in the blue light of the snapdragon flames. The fabric was charred but still intact, as far as he could tell. "Has your skin been burned?" he asked, stooping over her hand and wishing that there were more light in the room to see by.

"No," Emma said waspishly, "but I believe you have crushed my fingers."

Hugh glanced at her and smiled slightly before looking back to her hand and beginning to remove the glove gently, fingertip by fingertip.

"I was *very* close to picking up the almond, you know." Her voice was bitter, but he saw her dimple peep out as he looked up at her.

He held her bare hand in his, trying to ignore how soft her skin felt on his own. "In this dim light, I can't tell whether the skin is red." He glanced at the illuminated tree. "Come to the light of the tree. If you have been burned, we should treat it immediately."

She sighed dramatically.

"Please let us know if we may do anything to help," Miss Bolton said in a worried tone, as Alfred grabbed her hand in a comforting gesture.

Emma smiled at her and nodded, following Hugh to the tree.

Hugh stopped next to it, the branches brushing up against his coat as Emma joined him. The scent of pine wafted around them, overtaking the smell of burning firewood and brandy.

"Let us see what damage has been done," he said, holding out a hand to invite hers.

"I am quite all right," Emma insisted, though she offered her hand all the same, holding the charred glove in her other hand.

Hugh took her hand in his again, wishing that it were to keep hold of rather than for a brief inspection for injury. Where her hands were soft, delicate, and smooth, Hugh's were undoubtedly rough—hardly a pleasant experience for Emma. But it was decidedly pleasant for him to hold hers.

He examined her fingertips in the candlelight. "They don't look particularly red, which I would expect them to if you had been burned. Do they hurt?"

Emma shook her head. "And if you think this will keep me from the almond, you are horribly mistaken."

Hugh laughed and looked up from her hand.

Her eyes sparkled, the flame of numerous candles reflecting back at him. "And what if I obtain it before you?" He knew exactly what reward he would claim if he could; if things had been different.

What reward did *she* wish for?

Her gaze flitted down to her hand in his, but she made no move to pull it away.

"Then I suppose," she said, "that we must consider ourselves enemies once again and our truce at an end."

He brushed off the dismay he felt. He wasn't ready for Emma to revert to her icy enmity. How would he bear it after the last few days? "So, I must prepare myself to again face the infamous wrath of Miss Caldwell?"

She laughed but was prevented from responding.

"What a very thorough inspection you are doing, Hugh," said Alfred in a sharp voice.

Emma's hand dropped, and Hugh felt a flash of annoyance with Alfred.

He looked to his brother. He and Miss Bolton were no longer holding hands, and Miss Bolton's head was bowed and turned away from Alfred. Alfred wore a scowl.

Emma walked back over to them, and Hugh took in a breath and followed, sitting again on the chaise-lounge near her.

"No harm done," Emma said. "I believe this was all a pretense, though. Lieutenant Warrilow wishes to keep me from the almond, of course. But he shan't."

Alfred let out a scoff. "Yes, Hugh will stop at nothing to attain his goals, no matter the wreckage he leaves behind." He stood and stalked out of the room.

"Alfred," called out Miss Bolton, following after him.

Hugh sat motionless, stunned, a great lump in his throat that he couldn't even bring himself to swallow. What had happened so suddenly to alter the wonderful understanding between his brother and Miss Bolton?

To hear how Alfred felt about him, how he perceived him, it struck right at Hugh's core. No matter how many times it had seemed that his mistakes were finally behind him, Hugh found himself confronting them again and again.

He was vaguely aware of Emma's presence, of the fact that they were the only ones remaining in the candlelit room, but all he could manage was to drop his head into his hands.

What a mess had he made of his life and the lives of those he loved?

9

Emma forced herself to sit still, afraid that if she moved, she would draw attention to herself and to the fact that she and Lieutenant Warrilow were alone together in the dark room. Her impulses warred: one telling her to leave the room, to leave the lieutenant to himself, to pull away from the discomfort of being present with his strong emotions; the other impulse telling her to comfort the large man in front of her, who seemed to have crumpled at his brother's unkind words.

For so long, she had seen the lieutenant just as Alfred had described him: a man who acted out of self-interest, heedless of how it affected those around him.

But such a characterization did not account for the man who sat two feet away from her, silent and cast down. It didn't account for anything she had seen of him over the past few days. Whether there was some truth to it or none, she had to admit to herself that her opinion of him had been hastily modified and woefully inaccurate.

Casting her eyes away from the troubling image of the lieutenant's pain, she made a small movement to rise from the couch, to leave him with whatever emotion he needed to sort through. She had thought there would be some sense of justice to see him in pain. But there was nothing of that in what Emma felt.

Rather, in his hunched form and the hands which covered his face from her view, she caught a glimpse of Lucy. She had comforted Lucy in her dejection. Who would comfort the lieutenant?

She cleared her throat and scooted nearer, ignoring an impulse to put an understanding hand on his back, as she might have done for Lucy. "I am sure that your brother did not mean what he said, Lieutenant. He was only speaking out of anger. I understand that he and Miss Bolton are in a difficult position regarding their engagement, and it has him on edge, I imagine."

She shifted in her seat again. It was strange to be reassuring the man she had sworn she would always hate, to be contradicting the words she herself might have said only a week ago.

The lieutenant's hands moved down his face, pulling at his features and stretching his skin downward as he sat up, still not looking at her. "He spoke the truth, out of anger or not. I have only managed to bring hurt to those around me."

It took a moment for Emma to find any words to counter his statement. She had agreed with his sentiment for too long to have any contrary words at the ready. But she could hardly confirm what he had said—she was not so unkind.

And surely it wasn't entirely true, even if Emma didn't know how to respond. What might the lieutenant's mother say if she were here, in Emma's seat, comforting the son she loved?

"It is *not* true, though," Emma said.

He looked at her, a wry smile appearing at the corner of his mouth. "You needn't try to pretend you disagree, Miss Caldwell."

Emma was glad for the relative darkness of the room, feeling the heat seep into her cheeks.

"I am not pretending," she insisted. Seeing his incredulity, she continued. "I can think of a number of reasons it is untrue. Most notably, you bring your mother great joy. I have seen a contentment in her the past few days that was missing during the entirety of your absence. And your brother, too, despite the way he just lashed out at you. Besides that, think of what comfort you brought to the villagers earlier today."

"That was *your* idea," he said, though he seemed touched by her comments.

She waved away his words. "My initial idea, perhaps, but you were the one who made sure that it was carried out. It was *you* who insisted that it not be the servants who did so."

He rubbed at his mouth and shook his head. "I'm afraid that it hardly outweighs the pain I have caused elsewhere."

"I am sure it is nothing that cannot be forgiven or set right, Lieutenant."

"Then you haven't any idea of its scope." He paused. "Do you know that a man died to save me?" His voice was low and soft, and she watched his throat bob. "Did you know that, because of me, his wife and child are left without a husband or father?"

Her mouth opened wordlessly. "No," she finally said in a soft voice, looking down at her clasped hands, one still ungloved. "I did not know that. But surely he would not have sacrificed his own life if he thought you were not worth such a sacrifice."

"Robert Seymour would sacrifice himself for any man," the lieutenant said, staring into the lights on the tree.

Emma's head came up. "Robert Seymour?"

"You knew him?"

Emma nodded and closed her eyes. "I know his wife somewhat. I can tell you, though, that he wouldn't wish for you to be eaten up with guilt. He would want his sacrifice to *enable* your happiness, not to diminish it."

He frowned, reaching into his pocket and pulling out a signet ring, letting the candlelight reflect off the large red stone set within gold. "This belonged to Seymour. I have been meaning to return it to his wife, but"— he grimaced —"my courage fails me." He looked up from the ring at Emma, an earnest question in his eyes. "How can I face the woman who became a widow so that I could live?"

She wet her lips, unsure how to respond. His burden was not an easy one to live with, and Emma was too familiar with the Seymour's situation to downplay the emotional and financial difficulty they faced at the loss of Robert.

"It will not be easy, I'm sure. But perhaps returning the ring can put you in a situation to discover how else you might assist them. There is no doubt that they stand in need. But your guilt, understandable as it may be, serves no one—least of all you." She raised up her shoulders. "Let it spur you to action, let it drive you to make things better than they otherwise would be. You have the means to do much good."

He was watching her steadily, holding the signet ring between his thumb and forefinger and then clutching it in his fist. "You are right." He shut his eyes and exhaled. "But I will never be able to repay what he did for me."

Emma reached for his hand, covering it with hers. She felt his hand startle slightly as he looked at her with surprise.

The lieutenant clearly felt his share of pain and, much as Emma might have thought this fact would satisfy her and make her feel some sense of poetic justice existed, she found that, sitting with him here and hearing how he hurt, she only wished to comfort him, to help him see the good he had done.

"No," she said. "I don't think you will be able to repay it fully." She looked down at her hand on top of his. "But you saved another man's life, you gave him a home and work, and that means something, Lieutenant. It is no small thing to help another in their greatest need."

He stared into her eyes, his own soft and tender, a smile playing at the corner of his frowning mouth. "Never did I think to be consoled by you, Miss Caldwell."

She smiled teasingly at him. "I am only abiding by the terms of our truce, of course." She looked away, her smile fading slightly. "And despite what I may have given you to think, you have made my unexpected stay here *more* rather than less bearable."

She stole a glance at him, realizing suddenly how very close they were sitting to one another, how their hands still touched. She could feel the heat of his leg on her own, and she stood quickly, removing her hand from his.

He followed suit, picking up her charred glove and handing it to her. "Thank you for staying with me. I am sure this was not how you envisioned spending Christmas."

She gave a soft laugh. Would she have done things differently if she could have? Would she have escaped the conversation she'd just had with the lieutenant if given the opportunity?

No. She had seen a new side of the lieutenant—a side which drew her to him. What she was to do with such feelings, she didn't know. But she knew she wouldn't trade them.

The lieutenant reached for her shawl, draped across the back of the chaise, and placed it over her shoulders.

Emma felt her heart thump uncomfortably as his hands brushed her arms, his face near enough that she could feel his breath graze her cheek.

It was a polite gesture, no more, and yet her body was not reacting that way. Did he feel it, too?

Having wrapped the shawl around her shoulders, he stood looking down at her, still so near, and the distance between them thickened with tension.

She had to know if he felt it, and she looked into his eyes. They held affection and tenderness, and his warm, sweet breath filled the space between them. The air stilled in the room, making her thumping heart seem all the louder.

He leaned over slowly, and she closed her eyes, feeling his gentle lips meet hers and his hand cradle her cheek. Dizziness struck her, and she put an arm around his waist to steady her, her shawl dropping down to the floor. His own arm wrapped around her, bringing her close as the kiss became ardent and fervent, leaving them in a sort of reckless oblivion in the tree-lit room. There was nothing and no one but the two of them, no thoughts; nothing but the headiness and the breaking of tension that suddenly turned the kiss slow and sweet.

Emma broke away, pushing off his chest with her hands, stepping backward and blinking rapidly to set the world aright—to get a hold of herself.

She shook her head, slowly at first, then faster, avoiding the lieutenant's eyes.

"No." She shut her eyes. "This was a mistake."

She allowed herself one glance at him, at the hands which had held her firmly in their grip but now hung empty and limp at his side; at the piece of hair which had dropped down over his forehead in those few impassioned moments; at the eyes which watched her with confusion and hurt.

She rushed from the room.

THE TEMPERATURES ROSE RAPIDLY the day after Christmas, melting the once-icy snow in less than a day, making rivulets in the dirt roads which prevented Emma's departure until the following day.

She tried to focus on the relief that she felt upon seeing patches of grass appear on the lawns and hearing the drip of melting snow from the rooftop. She could go home!

She pushed aside the feeling of sadness that crept in around her relief, refusing to acknowledge it or the suspicion that it was centered around the lieutenant.

And the kiss she had shared with him? It was best not to think on it, as it brought on the strangest mix of giddiness and guilt and confusion—a combination that Emma felt wholly incapable of dealing with.

What had come over her? What had come over *him*?

She avoided him all day, taking her breakfast in her room and pleading the headache to avoid dinner with the family, even though her stomach growled with hunger as she waited for something to be brought to her room. She couldn't look him in the eye—she was too afraid of what she might see there if she did.

Did he regret the kiss? Had it simply been gratitude that he hadn't known how else to express? Or was there something behind it?

Truthfully, she didn't know that she could bear the answer to any of those questions, and seeing him would undoubtedly make it clear.

Emma was not the only one showing signs of melancholy. It had only required passing Alfred in the corridor to note his sullen demeanor and the despondent civility of Miss Bolton. With the thawing of the ice outdoors, all the cracks that had developed during their snowing-in—the ones they had ignored while the world stopped —seemed to have split open into deep, irreversible fissures.

The departure from Norfield the following morning had been a nerve-wracking experience for Emma. She knew that the entire family would gather in the courtyard to bid her farewell—that she would be obligated to face the lieutenant there, despite having successfully avoided him the entire day before.

But he was *not* there. And Emma was conscious of a crushing feeling of disappointment, which she tried to persuade herself was actually relief.

Did he not care that she was leaving? Had he been avoiding *her* all day as well?

She smiled and embraced Lady Dayton, determined to put what had happened at Norfield behind her, as much as she could. The odds of success for such a goal were doubtful, as she left with an invitation in hand, inviting her family to dine at Norfield in just three days' time.

Three days to decide how to act toward the lieutenant. Or would he absent himself from the dinner, too?

The roads were still muddy, but Emma's coachman Rhodes managed to bring her to Marsdon House in safety, all the same. By the time the carriage pulled into the courtyard, Emma's heart was pounding so forcefully that she wouldn't have been surprised if Lucy had heard it from inside the house. She stepped down into the mud—the only remnant of the undisturbed snow that had blanketed everything just two days ago.

When she came into the entry hall, she was accosted by three of her younger siblings, all eager to tell her just how much she had missed in her absence.

Lucy and Mr. Pritchard stood against the wall, patiently waiting for the little ones' attention to wane. Lucy's hand was on her chest, evidence of her relief at seeing Emma, and it was clear from her alert gaze that she was eager to speak with her sister. No doubt she was wondering how Emma had fared at Norfield where conversation would naturally have included Lieutenant Warrilow—the man she abhorred.

Had abhorred.

Emma swallowed nervously as her siblings ran off down the corridor. She almost called them back, simply to avoid the conversation she knew she must have. What could she say when her own feelings were so confused? When she had last left Lucy, she had been bemoaning the lieutenant's faulty character; she was returning now having gone so far in the opposite direction as to *kiss* the man? And to have enjoyed it? To have relived it a number of times, try as she might to forget it?

And Lucy still ignorant of the lieutenant's presence in England—still thinking he might be dead.

"Come, Emma," said Lucy, putting a hand out. "There is tea in the parlor."

Emma took Lucy's hand, and Mr. Pritchard bowed, allowing them to walk in front of him.

Emma hardly knew what they discussed as she sipped her tea. She only knew that Mr. Pritchard's departure from the parlor signaled the opportunity she required.

Both Emma's and Lucy's eyes followed him out of the room.

Lucy set down her teacup, letting out a sigh. "I am so relieved to know that you are well, Emma. I have worried and prayed so. I had to trust that you arrived at Norfield before the storm, for I couldn't bear the thought of you, stranded in some inn on the road home." She grimaced at Emma. "Though I am sure it was far from ideal to be stranded at Norfield for days on end."

Emma forced a smile. It *had* been ideal in many ways. But nothing like Emma thought it would be.

Lucy looked well. The blush in her cheeks was natural, and her eyes held a healthy glow. It gave Emma hope—hope that she wouldn't be shaken by knowing of Lieutenant Warrilow's return.

"How did you find Lord and Lady Dayt—"

"Lucy," Emma said, shutting her eyes to summon her strength.

Lucy went quiet, her eyebrows up.

Emma couldn't bear to postpone it any longer. If she did, she might lose her nerve. Lieutenant Warrilow's face swam before her, looking down at her, full of intensity in the moment before he had kissed her. Before she had kissed him back. She blinked away the image.

"Hugh Warrilow is home."

Lucy went still, staring at Emma uncomprehending. "What?"

Emma raised up her shoulders and exhaled through her nose. "He arrived home very unexpectedly the evening of my visit to Norfield." She swallowed. "He is alive."

Lucy swallowed. She said nothing, and Emma watched her sister with tension seizing her body. What was Lucy feeling? Relief? Hurt? Was she still in love with the lieutenant? Nausea swept over Emma as she waited.

Lucy's eyes pooled with tears, and Emma's heart sank.

A sob escaped Lucy, and her hand shot to her mouth as she rose from the couch. Turning on her heel, she ran from the room.

Emma sat, frozen in her chair. She took her top lip under her teeth. Should she follow?

No. How could she possibly comfort Lucy with the weight of all her own unspoken confusion pressing down on her conscience? If Lucy was overset by the knowledge that the lieutenant was home, what would be her reaction to discover all that had transpired during Emma's time there? What would she say to know that Emma had kissed the man that Lucy had yearned to marry?

Emma shuddered. She had made a terrible mistake. How in the world was she to face the lieutenant at dinner? And in the company of Lucy, no less?

LUCY HAD DONE a decent job of covering her shock and anguish by the time she dressed and descended the stairs to dinner. If Emma hadn't been such a close observer of Lucy's past pain, she might not have noticed anything was amiss. She was more somber than usual and quiet, even for her calm disposition. But overall, Lucy managed to smile and talk enough to prevent any questions about what was ailing her, all while Emma observed with a knot in the pit of her stomach.

When Emma managed to find a moment alone with her, Lucy had assured her that she shouldn't worry over her at all. "It was a shock, no more," she said, uninterested in further discussion. But her throat bobbed, and Emma didn't know how to believe her.

What if she were masking deep feelings of regret beneath her blanched but otherwise placid façade?

Flashbacks of Emma's time at Norfield intruded into her thoughts constantly—the truce, the snowball fight, the dejected lieutenant in need of comfort, the kiss.

The kiss.

How would she look at him without remembering the kiss? Without wondering what it meant to him? Without wondering what it would be like to repeat it?

And how would she ever explain to Lucy that she no longer hated the lieutenant but admired him, respected him, and cared for him—cared for him she knew not how much?

✻ 10 ✻

Hugh stood in the Seymours' drawing room, his foot tapping nervously on the tattered rug below. His hand shot to his jacket to the distinctive lump where Seymour's ring sat in his pocket.

Of course it was still there. He had checked more than once on the carriage ride to be sure he hadn't forgotten it. The ring was the only thing keeping him from feeling brazen for even daring to set foot there, after all. His only consolation was that his anxiety had temporarily overtaken the incessant and overwhelming despondency which had been threatening to overtake him since Emma's departure.

The door opened, and Mrs. Seymour walked in, holding a toddler on her hip and trailed by two other young children.

Hugh's jaw shifted, and he suppressed the impulse to squeeze his eyes shut. There was something even more harrowing about seeing the widow and children Seymour left behind than there had been in watching Seymour draw his last breath.

Mrs. Seymour looked bone-weary. The shawl she wore over her arms was threadbare, and the children's clothing pressed but stained. Hugh knew Robert had never been well-to-do—a country barrister, no more—but it was clear that his family was in difficult financial straits.

The children looked up at Hugh with large, wary eyes.

Not wanting to frighten the children, he winked at them. A responsive smile peeped at the corner of the oldest girl's mouth before being swiftly hidden.

Mrs. Seymour smiled at him, as well, but it didn't eliminate the sorrow in her eyes. "Hello, Lieutenant," she said, motioning for him to take a seat. "Please have a seat."

He sat down on the edge of the upholstered chair. "I am honored to meet you, Mrs. Seymour," he said, clearing his throat. "I won't take much of your valuable time, I assure you, but I couldn't neglect to pay you a visit."

She sat down. "I confess I was surprised when I received your note. But you served with Robert, didn't you? I remember your name from some of his letters."

Hugh nodded. "Robert was in my regiment. An exceptional soldier and a man I endeavor to emulate." His voice broke slightly, and he cleared it again. "I think you cannot be aware that the fatal injury he sustained occurred in his efforts to protect me." His jaw shifted from side to side as his mind returned to that day in Vitoria, their regiment lining the banks of the Zadorra river. He blinked to dispel the smell of gunfire, the sound of sabers clashing, and the image of blood-stained ground. "There was a soldier I hadn't seen—a French one. If Robert hadn't seen him..." He clenched his jaw, willing himself to look Mrs. Seymour in the eyes. She deserved that much, at least—that the man responsible for her husband's death should meet her gaze. "He saved my life."

Mrs. Seymour was rigid in her seat, the toddler she held in her arms moving constantly, as tears made little streams down her cheeks. She said nothing, only nodding with a trembling chin.

Hugh swallowed. "Before Robert's body was taken for burial, I took the liberty of removing this"— he extracted the ring from his pocket and held it out to Mrs. Seymour —"from his finger. I know how proud Robert was of his name, and I stood in no doubt whatsoever of how well he loved you and your children. He spoke of you often."

Mrs. Seymour took the ring from his hand and stared at it for a moment. A sob escaped her, and she stifled it with a hand as her oldest daughter—hardly seven years old, surely—came and took the toddler from her arms.

A little boy who Hugh judged to be about six years old walked over to his mother and peered at the ring she held between her thumb and forefinger. He looked up at Hugh.

"My papa gave it to you?"

Hugh pursed his lips in an effort to control his emotions and nodded. He rested his elbows on his knees and leaned toward the boy. "You look very much like your papa. He was a valiant man, and he saved me. Never forget that."

A sniffle came from the girl holding the toddler. She bounced up and down as the boy whined, but there were tears on her cheeks. She looked at Hugh with anger and hurt. "But I didn't want him to save you! I wanted him to come home!"

"Liza!" Mrs. Seymour said, her own voice shaky but chastising.

Hugh shook his head, glancing at Mrs. Seymour to convey his understanding. He waited a moment until the catch in his throat subsided. He looked Liza in the eye. "If I could trade places with your father and bring him back to you, I would do it in a heartbeat. He was a better man than I have ever been."

The toddler began crying, and Mrs. Seymour motioned for Eliza to bring him back to her. Eliza handed him over and wiped at her tears with an impatient brush of her hand.

Her younger brother came to stand beside her, looked up at her watering eyes and began crying softly.

"Perhaps it would be best if you left, Lieutenant," Mrs. Seymour said with a teary grimace. "We have many things to attend to today— we have had to let go all but two of the servants. I am sure you understand." She sniffed and motioned for her children to gather in her arms. She wore the signet ring on her thumb.

Hugh nodded and stood. Bowing deeply, he took one last look at Mrs. Seymour, arms around her children, and let himself out of the house.

Hugh sat bleary-eyed in front of the Christmas tree, every other candle in the room extinguished. Only a few, sporadic flames were left speckling the Christmas tree. He had insisted that the tree be left up and at least partially lit until all the decorations were taken down on Epiphany.

The few lights looked fuzzy, and he watched as they reflected off the decanter of brandy in front of him—brandy from the same bottle they had used to play snapdragon a week ago.

What a fool he had been to come home—to think that he could somehow move beyond his past so easily and mend what he had broken. All he had managed to do was create more pain.

Hugh put a hand to his coat, feeling the absence of the signet ring. Young, tearful eyes hovered in his vision, as if he needed another reminder of the destruction he had caused. Those children didn't want to hear how valiant their father was. They wanted him alive and well. They needed him.

No one needed Hugh.

He hadn't missed the evidence of the straits the Seymour family was in. How would they fare without a father? How would Mrs. Seymour make do with several young children to feed and clothe? With hardly any help from servants?

And Hugh the reason for their hardship.

He set his glass of brandy down, rubbing his forehead harshly. There must be something more he could do for them than to simply return Robert's ring, telling tales of his bravery. Hadn't Emma said as much? He had a responsibility toward them, but he doubted that

Mrs. Seymour wanted much to do with him. He would only be a reminder of what she had lost.

He sat up straight, his eyes wide and staring.

There *was* one thing he might do. Of course, it was paltry, all things considered. But surely something was better than nothing?

He would need to write to his uncle and request a meeting. It would only be right to get his permission first.

He leapt to his feet, putting a hand to his forehead and blinking rapidly as the dizziness set in from the drink. Once the room stabilized, he took a candle from the mantle above the fireplace and lit it using one from the tree before striding down the corridor to the library.

Flipping his coat tails out and seating himself, he grabbed for a sheet of paper and a quill, scratching away on the parchment, blinking to keep his eyes focused.

He doubted his uncle would deny his wish, but he needed to speak with him, all the same. Perhaps he would even have some words of wisdom regarding Alfred's situation.

And heaven knew how much Hugh needed wisdom.

EMMA HAD DRESSED for the dinner party at Norfield with trembling hands, unable to quench a wish to look her best—it was a silly inclination, but not one she could deny. She felt a little boost of confidence, wearing her favorite white crepe dress with its cascade of pale green spangles down the front, as she stepped up the stairs to Norfield, trailing behind her family.

The Warrilows were in the drawing room, and Emma's heart skipped a beat as her eyes fell upon Lieutenant Warrilow.

He was there. And his brown eyes found her almost as quickly as her eyes found him. Did that mean something?

Her body stilled, but her heart raced as she met his gaze for a moment, wishing she could read his expression and know his thoughts.

She hardly knew whether or not she wanted to witness the reunion between the lieutenant and Lucy, but she couldn't have avoided it without incivility. Lucy was arm-in-arm with Mr. Pritchard, but she took Emma by the hand in an urgent gesture Emma recognized as a request for support.

Lucy managed to keep her composure admirably, only her heightened color and the tightness of her grip on Emma's arm betraying her inner agitation.

Lieutenant Warrilow was all kind politeness, genuine in his congratulations to Lucy and Mr. Pritchard. Emma could see the apology written in his gaze, whether or not Lucy noticed it. She hoped that seeing Lucy would set his mind at ease, knowing that she would be taken care of—that his actions had been but a temporary adversity. He needn't continue to berate himself for what he had done.

Emma conversed and listened with as much focus as she could muster, but her preoccupation wouldn't let her mind rest. She wanted to speak with the lieutenant but dreaded it at the same time. Would Lucy perceive the battle going on in Emma's mind and heart if she saw them together? Surely, she would at least notice the lack of strain and wonder at it—wonder at the fact that Emma had said nothing of the change.

It wasn't until the men joined the women in the drawing room that the opportunity to interact with the lieutenant was granted.

Emma was standing before the Christmas tree, reaching to one of the cream paper flowers she had helped fold, when the lieutenant came up beside her. Her heart stuttered, and she glanced at Lucy who stood across the room, speaking with her mother and Lady Dayton.

"Is our truce at an end, then?" he said, adjusting one of the flowers that had sunk deep into the tree's branches.

The truce? She had forgotten the truce.

It had only motivated her behavior toward him for a day or two. It had been a needed catalyst, to be sure, putting her in a place where she could see past her prejudice against the lieutenant.

But it had not been a determining factor—or even a conscious one—in her behavior toward him for some time now.

"Is there any need for a truce?" she finally said, her mind flitting back to the last time they had stood in the light of the Christmas tree, his arm wrapped around her waist and a hand on her cheek, gentle and then pressing.

"I admit that I had hoped there was not."

She glanced at him, and he met her gaze squarely. How could she stop from reading into every single thing he said?

Her eyes darted to Lucy.

Lucy. She had to remember Lucy. It didn't matter what the lieutenant meant. It didn't matter if he regretted the kiss—a thought which made her stomach feel sick—or wished to repeat it—a thought which made Emma's head reel.

"She is still in love with you." She looked up at him.

A frown descended upon his face as he glanced toward Lucy. "How can you be sure?"

Her shoulders came up in a helpless gesture. "I hadn't gone further than telling her that you were alive and at Norfield when she buried her face in her hands and fled the room. She has been"— she took in a breath, searching for the word —"different ever since."

Lieutenant Warrilow took in a deep breath. "It must have been a great shock to her."

"Yes," Emma said softly, "that is what she claims."

Emma's eyes moved to Alfred. He looked strangely exposed without Miss Bolton at his side. His brow was drawn, just as it had been since he had left the room in his Christmas evening outburst. But far from the energy and anger of that evening, there was a beaten and conquered air about his sober expression.

"Has Miss Bolton returned home then?" Emma asked, glad for a reason to change the subject.

Hugh rubbed his chin and nodded. "It is as we suspected. When Alfred requested an audience with her father to inform him of his change in fortunes, it did not end well. Mr. Bolton has insisted that his daughter be released from the engagement."

"How terrible for them both." Emma's mouth twisted to the side, and she looked up at the lieutenant. There was so much pain among them. She looked again to Lucy, whose eyes were on them, an unreadable expression on her face.

Emma attempted a smile at her, knowing that it was a feeble one. Lucy would find it strange to see Emma and Lieutenant Warrilow side-by-side.

Mr. Pritchard touched Lucy's arm, and her eyes lingered for a moment on Emma and the lieutenant, even as her head turned toward her fiancé.

"Will you return to town after the holidays?" the lieutenant asked.

Emma shut her eyes. A return to town meant facing the impending offer of marriage from Mr. Douglas—a prospect which made her stomach feel leaden. How had her feelings undergone such a rapid and full transformation?

"I believe so," she said. "And you?"

He shook his head, and she was conscious of an overwhelming feeling of disappointment.

"I have things to take care of here."

It made sense, of course, that he needed to stay at Norfield. He had been gone for three years, after all. And it was silly to expect him to follow her to London. But, for some reason, his words pierced her as evidence that her regard was not returned—that he had no desire to spend time with her now that circumstances didn't make it an inevitability, now that the snow had melted.

Did he realize that, if they ever saw one another again, she would likely be engaged or married to Mr. Douglas?

She swallowed, feeling a need to provoke some reaction out of him, to discover what he really felt. If she had truly been brave, she might have asked him forthrightly. But she hadn't the nerve. "I understand," she said, clasping her fingers to keep them from trembling, "that Mr. Douglas has some intention of calling upon my father when we return."

It was feeble. It made her cringe to hear herself say it. It sounded desperate to her own ears and likely felt unfeeling and arrogant to his.

She looked at him, at his flared nostrils, his stiff posture.

"Then I wish you every happiness, Miss Caldwell." He bowed and walked from the room, leaving her behind with glazed eyes and something very much like a hole in her chest.

11

Hugh stalked out of the drawing room, closing the door behind him and heading for the front door. Stepping into the cold night air, he kicked at the nearby bush, its brown leaves surrendering and crumbling to the ground as he combed his fingers through his hair.

In the stillness of the outside air, his pulse began to calm.

He shut his eyes and bowed his head, shaking it slowly. He couldn't rid himself of the look in Emma's eyes as he had left her side —powerless anguish. He hadn't meant to be so curt with her, but the thought of her marrying this Mr. Douglas?

His fingernails dug into the palms of his hands.

It was unbearable.

Whatever disappointment he thought he had endured upon leaving behind all hope for a chance with Emma when he had gone off to war, it paled in comparison to the disappointment of having that chance in front of him, within reach, and then losing it all over again.

He blew out a breath. The puff expanded around him and dissipated in the midnight air.

He had thought himself changed after his time fighting in the war —ready to accept the duty and consequences that had felt like burdens before.

Why, then, did he find it so difficult to confront the idea that losing Emma was yet another consequence of the decision he had made three years ago? That there had never really been a chance with her?

He had known it before, and yet he had been foolhardy enough to jump at the chance when it so unexpectedly was presented. Or *seemed* to be presented. He had foolishly taken a few moments of her kindness and comfort as evidence that she cared for him as he cared for her.

She no longer hated him, but it did not follow that she loved him.

He had to remind himself of that. Day in, day out, until he accepted it.

But the kiss they had shared? He squeezed his eyes shut, trying to dispel the memory.

It made no sense.

For Hugh, it had been the materialization of a long wished-for dream. An ecstatic moment that he had despaired of ever experiencing.

But for Emma?

He kicked at the bush again, more softly this time.

Had he fooled himself into thinking that she had returned the embrace?

No. He couldn't have imagined the way her arms had wrapped around him, or the way her soft lips had pressed to his.

But *she* had pulled away. Pushed, really. She had said it was a mistake.

He was a fool. Things were so much simpler on campaign.

He pressed on his shoulder. It was irritating him much less since the frigid cold had subsided. He felt more confident than ever that it might heal completely within a few weeks, though he had anticipated a much longer leave.

His regiment would welcome him back—he had no doubt about that. But was he ready to stake his life again, ready for life at war again, so soon after returning home? A return to the Continent would mean forfeiting—or at least postponing—the good deed he wished to do for the Seymours.

What would his father say to learn that he was considering a return already? Would it rekindle Alfred's hope in a match with Miss Bolton? Would Alfred secretly be hoping for Hugh's death and a second chance with the woman he loved?

Hugh folded his arms, staring out at the tree-lined drive. He couldn't stay at Norfield. But neither did he feel he could leave and return to the war-torn continent, with all its memories, many of which were anything but pleasant. There were unpleasant memories everywhere. There was guilt and pain everywhere.

He frowned and rubbed the back of his neck with a firm hand, remembering Emma's words to him about the crushing guilt he labored under.

"Let it spur you to action, let it drive you to make things better than they otherwise would be. You have the means to do much good."

She was right. It did no good for him to wallow in shame and guilt. Returning the ring to the Seymours had been difficult enough. But surely there was more he could do. Emma had been right: he stood in a position to help the Seymours, and he sincerely hoped that his uncle's visit would make that a reality.

HUGH STOOD with his hands behind his back, feeling the warmth of the shaft of afternoon sunlight which illuminated a piece of the Norfield courtyard through a temporary gap in the clouds.

Lord Siddington stepped down from his yellow chaise with a bounce. He was on the shady side of fifty, but no one would have guessed as much to look at him. Lean, energetic, and dressed more like a fop than a man in his middle age, he exuded youth until closer inspection revealed the small lines forming around his mouth, on his forehead, and at the corners of his eyes, concealed with a fair amount of makeup.

After the scandal with Lucy, Lord Siddington hadn't hesitated to offer the purchase of a commission for Hugh.

"In my day," he had said to a grave Hugh three years ago, "we did a tour of the Continent, my boy, but with Boney still on the loose, I'm afraid the closest you'll get is letting me buy you a pair of colors. Never had an ounce of desire for the army myself, but it seems I never come upon a young man these days but he's army-mad. It might do you good to get away, you know—exhaust your anger on the frogs instead of staying here with that dashed Friday face you're wearing."

Uncle Sid, as Hugh was wont to call him, was as free with his money as he was with his gossip, and he had always had a soft spot for Hugh.

"Hugh, dear boy!" he said now, grinning widely and handing his malacca cane to the postilion so that he could properly embrace his nephew. "Thought you'd stuck your spoon in the wall. Devilish glad to hear it's not the case."

Hugh smiled appreciatively, heartily embracing his uncle. Alfred couldn't stand the man, but Hugh never failed to be entertained in his presence.

"No," he said, "I came close a few times, but I'm still here."

They pulled apart, and Lord Siddington took his cane back from the postilion. He leaned in toward Hugh, saying, "Carried a cane for years because it was *de rigueur,* but the truth is, I'm beginning to need it, my boy." He shook his head. "Devilish thing it is, getting old. Never thought it would happen to me." He laughed and slapped Hugh on the back.

Hugh chuckled and stepped in line with his uncle toward the house. "There is a matter I have been meaning to speak with you—"

Lord Siddington waved his hand and shook his head. "No, no, my boy. I have no intention of discussing business until I have a glass of whatever your father has been hiding in that marvelous cellar of his."

Once Lord Siddington had a glass of sherry in hand, the two of them sat down in the library, Uncle Sid stretching his legs out in front of him and crossing them at the ankles.

"Now," he said with a contented sigh, "what is it you wished to speak with me about?"

Knowing his uncle's short attention span, Hugh quickly related his interactions with Robert Seymour during their time in the same regiment, ending in Seymour's untimely death and the severely straitened circumstances his wife and children found themselves living in.

Lord Siddington frowned and shook his head. "A terrible shame. Seen it time and time again this past twenty years."

"Fortunately," Hugh said, "I came to an idea of how Mrs. Seymour and her children might be helped. It affects you, though, which is why I asked you here."

Lord Siddington's drink paused halfway between the table and his mouth, his eyes suddenly wary. "What sort of idea? I have no thought of marrying, my boy, so please—"

Hugh reared back and chuckled. "The notion never even occurred to me, though I do think you could do much worse than marrying Mrs. Seymour, if it came down to it. A few children at your heels might do you some good."

His uncle's eyes broadened, and he choked on his drink. "Heaven help me!" He set his drink down, pulling out a yellow spotted handkerchief and patting his lips with it. "I'd rather buy myself a pair of colors than submit to these ideas of yours."

Hugh shrugged. "It is your affair, of course. My idea, though, relates to your having purchased my commission in the first place. I have some thought of selling out, particularly if prospects improve and there is any likelihood of the war ending. I intended to return the money to you if I ever took such a step." He watched his uncle carefully.

"Good heavens," his uncle said. "What should I want with the money? No, my boy, it was a gift. The money is yours to do with as you please."

Hugh let out a small sigh of relief. "I intend to give the funds directly—and anonymously—to Mrs. Seymour when I do sell out. In the meantime, I hope that my mother and father will lend their support, given what the family sacrificed so that I might be here at all."

"Very noble, my boy, very noble," said Lord Siddington distractedly, picking up the decanter of sherry and inspecting it with narrowed eyes. "Richard always lays his hands on the very best of it!"

Hugh sighed at his uncle's inability to focus on anything of real importance.

"I suppose you've heard of Alfred's broken engagement?" he said, leaning back in his chair and resting his chin on his knuckles.

"Yes," Lord Siddington said, only half-listening. "Must be something in the air at Norfield."

Hugh frowned. "What do you mean?"

"Engagements being broken left and right in this house," he said, pouring himself another glass. "I'll tell you what, my boy. Don't get engaged in the first place. That's the ticket!"

"In this case," Hugh said, "it was not Alfred who broke the engagement. Not having heard from me in months, he and my parents were under the impression that Alfred would be inheriting. It was with such an understanding that Miss Bolton's father countenanced the engagement. My return has caused him to withdraw his support and insist Miss Bolton be released from the arrangement."

"Slippery fellow, eh?"

"Yes, but I think he might be persuaded to reconsider the match if only we could find some situation for Alfred."

Hugh paused, and Lord Siddington took out his tortoise-shell snuff box, opening it with a flick of the finger.

"His hope," Hugh continued, "was to seek the living at Balmaker, but he ceased doing so when he believed that there was no longer any need for him to find such employment, and the living was given to someone else."

Lord Siddington was rubbing a spot off his quizzing glass, taking little interest in the conversation—a fact that Hugh partially attributed to his relative indifference toward Alfred.

"I was hoping you might know of another situation that would suit?"

Lord Siddington put away his snuff box. The silence continued.

Lord Siddington gave a start, seeming to realize something was expected of him. "Eh? Yes, yes, very much a gentleman is Alfred."

Hugh suppressed a smile. "Uncle, I had asked whether you knew of any livings that Alfred might obtain, as the one at Balmaker is now occupied?"

"Oh," he said, astounded, "did you?" He frowned a moment. "You know, I just may. Lord Dunhaven's man at Keldale kicked the bucket last week, as I understand, and Dunhaven owes me more favors than he'll ever be able to repay. Towed him out of the river tick more than once, among other things." He shot Hugh a significant look and cleared his throat.

Hugh sat up straighter in his chair. "And you would be willing to call in one of those favors on Alfred's behalf?"

His uncle shrugged. "Might as well have a Warrilow there as some uppity country bumpkin."

"Alfred would do a wonderful job. The living at Keldale is significant, is it not?"

Lord Siddington pursed his lips. "Yes, I believe it comes with the living at Newmarsh, as well. The vicar—may he rest in peace—employed a curate there, of course, since it's devilish out of the way. Middle of nowhere, really. All told, I think the two livings would bring in somewhere in the range of five or six-hundred pounds."

Hugh sighed his relief. With the unentailed land Alfred would receive, such a position would allow him to get along quite comfortably. And it might just be enough to convince Miss Bolton's father to reconsider. Much as the man wished her to marry well, he had a great dislike of scandal, and informing everyone of the ended engagement would be sure to cause undesirable gossip—something he wished to keep as far away from his daughter as possible.

Hugh settled back into his chair, his mind hard at work, while Lord Siddington leaned back and shut his eyes.

Lord Siddington only intended to remain at Norfield for the night, a fact which had made Hugh raise his brows, having seen the abundance of valises and portmanteaux which the servants had taken up the stairs. But he agreed that he would write to Lord Dunhaven without delay and inform Hugh of the result as soon as he had a response.

Knowing that there was hope for Alfred's situation relieved a great burden from Hugh's shoulders. It would still be an adjustment, of course. It was only natural. For a time, Alfred had thought that he would be heir to a much larger fortune than the living he might be given at Keldale and Newmarsh.

But if it enabled him to marry Miss Bolton, Hugh felt that his brother would be content with the situation.

Hugh resolved not to speak to Alfred of the possibility until Lord Dunhaven's response arrived, but he took hope from his uncle's certitude in speaking of calling in the favor.

His own situation was less easily settled. The thought of remaining at Norfield, so near to Emma, knowing that marriage to her was an impossibility—it was an oppressive and intolerable prospect. But he had come home with a silent promise to himself that he would face his past and his future with courage, and to run from Norfield would be in direct contradiction to that oath.

No, he would not flee to war this time. He would sell his commission and give the money to the Seymours, then put his head down in learning the business of the estate.

Perhaps his father would allow him to manage things at Grindleham. He had only ever been there twice, and his few memories were of a small, overgrown property, but it would give him vital distance as well as practice in the upkeep of an estate in great need.

He made his way down the stairs at Norfield, pausing as he heard the voice of his mother and another woman, coming toward him from down the corridor.

He stepped onto the landing and leaned over for a view of the visitor.

It was Lucy.

She glanced at him as they approached, smiling, though not in the shy, hesitant way she had smiled at him in days past. It was more of a knowing smile, and it made his cravat feel tight.

What did she know that he didn't? And why had she come —alone?

He greeted her quickly and then moved down the corridor, taking a moment to look through the window at the grounds of Norfield until his mother had bid her goodbye.

The rhythmic footsteps of his mother's approach sounded, and he turned to her.

"Mama," he said, coming to her side to join her in her walk back toward the morning room. "What was that about?"

Her mouth broke into a smile, and she patted him on the arm. "A *private* chat with Lucy."

His head came back slightly. "How very mysterious," he said, feeling a prick of annoyance.

"Not mysterious, my dear, but not something I am free to communicate. It isn't for me to tell." She stopped in the doorway of the morning room and faced him, looking at him with all the love and warmth of a mother in her eyes. She reached her hand up and put it on his cheek. "Don't lose heart, Hugh." She held his eyes for a moment and then turned into the morning room.

🐾 I 2 🐾

Emma straightened the kissing bough hanging from the doorway for what seemed like the hundredth time. It was useless, really. It hadn't been hung properly, and whoever had made it had bunched the holly too densely on one side, adding to its imbalance.

But anything that could keep her thoughts and hands occupied was welcome to Emma. It had taken every ounce of her energy not to let despair consume her; to put on a pleasant smile in company; to entertain her younger siblings when all she wished to do was lie in bed, left to her unpleasant thoughts.

Of course, Lucy could know nothing of what was driving down Emma's spirits, so Emma had to find a way to be content with the assurance that her own pain was worth preventing the pain Lucy might have felt, had she known everything. And yet, it was but little balm on Emma's wounds.

She found herself falling into distracted fits, wondering how the lieutenant was faring, shuddering as she remembered the injured way he had looked at her when she had last seen him. He hadn't returned to the drawing room after their conversation, and Emma had remarked Lady Dayton's anxious glances at the door he had left through.

Of course, no one would have batted an eye to know that Emma and the lieutenant were on the outs.

Emma hadn't the energy or desire to set aright anyone's understanding. There was little point to such an endeavor, after all.

She gave the bough a little spin, surrendering to its insistence on chaos, and watched it dazedly.

"Emma?"

Emma blinked twice and looked down from the kissing bough to where Lucy stood in front of her, her hands clasped and hanging down in front of her, like the cream shawl she wore.

"May I speak with you a moment?"

Emma's eyebrows went up, and she nodded, stepping down from the stool. They walked over to the settee, Emma curling her legs underneath her and Lucy sitting up straight, her hands still clasped in her lap.

Emma looked at Lucy expectantly, trying to suppress the anxious feelings she felt churning in her stomach as she wondered what Lucy wished to say.

Lucy was silent, looking at her hands for a moment. "You are miserable, Emma," she finally said.

Emma opened her mouth wordlessly and then bit her lip. "I am *not* miserable." Her words sounded unpersuasive even to herself.

"Emma"— Lucy grimaced, something very near pity in her eyes —"surely you didn't think I wouldn't notice such a change in you? I had hoped you would confide in me, but I see you don't intend to, and I think I know why."

Emma's heart picked up speed. She was treading dangerous ground, but she hadn't any idea how to redirect the conversation without causing further suspicion.

"It is very like you to be so concerned for me"— Emma reached for one of Lucy's hands and squeezed it affectionately —"but you need not worry."

Lucy rubbed Emma's palm with her thumb, her eyes down. "You are in love with Hugh Warrilow, aren't you?"

Emma froze, swallowing the lump in her throat.

What could she say? Her conscience balked at the thought of lying to Lucy. But to affirm it would be to hurt her irrevocably.

Lucy shook her head, still not meeting Emma's eyes. "You needn't respond. I knew it when I saw you together the other night."

Emma was suddenly very aware of her breathing, as if the way her body wished to breathe would only betray her. She extracted her hand from Lucy's and rubbed a finger absently along the blue floral fabric of the settee. "It is true," she said carefully, "that I no longer hold him in aversion."

Lucy smiled wanly and looked at Emma. "A significant understatement, Emma."

Emma's finger stilled. She shut her eyes tightly and gripped her lips together. "It is of no account, Lucy. I plan to accept Mr. Douglas when he offers for me."

"Why on earth would you do such a thing?" Lucy said, straightening.

Emma stared at her. She could hardly say, *Because you are still in love with him.*

"Lucy," she said, taking in a deep breath and shaking her head, "your reaction upon discovering he had returned...." Her brows came together, and she shrugged. "I would never wish to hurt you."

Lucy shook her head. "It was a shock, Emma. For months, I had assumed he was dead, had despaired for poor Lady Dayton." She inclined her head. "I admit that, when I saw him again at Norfield, I wondered if perhaps I *did* still love him. And naturally I do admire him and shall always wish him well—"

Emma stifled her hopeful feelings, reminding herself that Lucy was as self-sacrificing as anyone she knew. She couldn't allow Lucy to make herself a martyr.

"—but I no sooner saw the two of you together than I realized how utterly meant for one another you are."

Emma looked up and then shook her head rapidly, taking Lucy's hand back into hers. "I could never hurt you in such a way, Lucy. After all you've been through."

"I am *well*, Emma." She gave a smile tinged with sadness. "Mr. Pritchard is a good, amiable gentleman, and I know that I shall have a good life with him." She inclined her head in a gesture of acknowledgment. "What I feel for him is nothing like the youthful passion I felt for Lieutenant Warrilow, to be sure. But I *do* love him. Only in a more staid and peaceful way. And that suits me better, I think."

Emma said nothing, but she found herself in private agreement.

Lucy had always been calm and gentle, constant and loyal. She betrayed none of the explosive emotion that plagued Emma. Lucy's reaction to Hugh's decision not to marry her had been uncharacteristically intense and turbulent. Emma had taken it as evidence of the depth of her love for him. But perhaps it was rather a testament to the unsuitability of their characters.

"And what's more, Emma"— Lucy held Emma's eyes and added her other hand to their clasped ones —"I could never live with myself knowing that, for my sake, you turned down an offer of marriage from a gentleman not only eminently eligible"— she smiled enigmatically at Emma —"but one who adores you and whom you adore equally."

Emma's lower lip trembled, and she took it between her teeth to control it.

"I mean it," Lucy said firmly.

"I couldn't bear it if something or someone came between us." She dashed away a tear from her cheek.

Lucy tilted her head to the side and looked at Emma with sincerity burning in her eyes. "I would never allow such a thing to happen. We are sisters, now and always."

She smiled and took Emma's free hand, bringing it together with the others so that all four hands cradled each other. "I went to Norfield yesterday," Lucy said, "and I spoke with Lady Dayton."

Emma's head came back, and she frowned. "Why?"

Lucy's smile widened. "When I saw you and the lieutenant at the dinner party, saw the way you looked at each other..." her shoulders came up. "I had to know if my suspicions were correct."

Emma swallowed, feeling her muscles tighten and her heart skip. "What suspicions?" She tried to infuse her voice with less burning curiosity than she felt, pulling one hand from Lucy's so that she could play distractedly with the knitting of her shawl—to avoid Lucy's eyes.

"Emma," said Lucy softly, a wondering light in her eyes, "did you know that Lieutenant Warrilow has been in love with you for years? That his feelings for you were the primary reason that he didn't feel that he could offer for me?"

Emma's fingers froze, and she looked up at Lucy, her voice catching in her throat.

It couldn't be.

Lucy nodded, as if she knew Emma doubted her words. "It is true, Emma."

Emma's eyelids fluttered, and Lucy's face swam strangely in front of her. She blinked, putting a hand on the settee to stabilize herself.

Hope sprang up inside her chest, only to be checked immediately. What was it doing to Lucy to say this? To know that Emma was the reason behind all the hurt she had gone through?

Lucy shook her head with a soft laugh. "I should have recognized it, Emma. And looking back, I can see it clearly. But I was too blinded by my own infatuation back then. It was selfish of me."

"Lucy," Emma said, her eyes stinging yet again, "I had no idea."

"No, I am sure you didn't. You are far too blind to your own qualities to have perceived the state of things." Lucy smiled wryly at her.

Emma fingered the edges of the shawl. "Everything you went through, Lucy"— she squeezed her eyes shut —"I would never have wished that upon you, never have wished to be the cause of it."

Lucy dropped her hand, wrapping her arms around Emma in a tight embrace and whispering in her ear, "It has all worked out for the best, in the end. I would go through it all again to know that it meant you would find someone to love." She pulled away from Emma, her eyes shimmering with tears amidst her smile.

"And now that that is settled," she said prosaically, wiping her eye with the back of her thumb, "I think you must go, with haste, to see the lieutenant and inform him in no uncertain terms that you return his regard."

Emma clenched her teeth. She still refused to believe that it was real—that the lieutenant loved her. That he had loved her for all these years. It seemed impossible. Too good to be true.

"What if you are wrong, Lucy?"

Lucy shook her head decidedly. "I am not. Lady Dayton stood in no doubt of her son's feelings—indeed, she expressed surprise more than once that *you* had not been aware of the state of his heart."

Emma's mind darted back to a conversation with Lady Dayton.

"You don't *know, then,"* she had said.

Is this what she had meant?

"In any case," Lucy said, "it seems that you have been ignorant of your regard for one another—something that is quite easily rectified, I think." She stood from the couch, pulling Emma up with her. "Come. I will see you off."

Enthusiasm and excitement buzzed from Lucy, but Emma stood still, resisting the tugging on her hand.

Lucy turned back, frowning and scanning Emma's face. "What is it? Do you not wish to see him?"

Emma gripped her lips together. She wanted nothing more than to undo the hurt she had caused when she had seen him last. The thought of seeing the lieutenant made her skin tingle and her heart thump wildly.

"Tell me, Emma. Have I misjudged your feelings?"

Emma pictured the lieutenant's eyes: all the times they had looked on her during her stay at Norfield. She had been too afraid to put a word to what she had seen in his eyes, too unwilling to believe it, too uncertain of what she herself was feeling.

She shook her head, unable to quench the smile that demanded expression. "No. Let us go."

❧ 13 ❧

Hugh instructed his valet to pack another pair of his sturdiest pantaloons. He anticipated that he would be spending a fair amount of time conversing with the bailiff at Grindleham and very little time at balls and parties.

His father's acquiescence to his request had been somewhat tortuously obtained. Lord Dayton's first response was to ask what Hugh was running from again.

Hugh had carefully explained that he wished to learn the ropes of estate management in a place requiring a more hands on approach than Norfield.

"Here at Norfield," he had argued, "I would learn maintenance of an estate already well-cared for. At Grindleham, I shall be required to get my hands a little dirty in arranging things, to become familiar with all the minor matters which can make or break an estate. I think it will stand me in better stead when the time comes for me to take over at Norfield."

His father had frowned upon hearing this. "I have been meaning to visit Grindleham for some time now, but for one reason or another,

I haven't ever found the time. I suppose you *could* make yourself useful there."

With a little more convincing on Hugh's part, the matter had been settled, and Hugh had taken to preparations without delay.

He heard the muffled rumbling of carriage wheels and pulled back one of the curtains. There was no mistaking the chaise coming down the drive: bright yellow and pulled by matched bays.

Hugh let the curtain fall back in place and strode quickly from his room, down the corridor and the staircase.

He had been waiting to hear from his uncle, but he had expected a letter rather than a visit. Was Lord Siddington's arrival in person to be viewed as a positive or negative omen for Alfred?

Small snowflakes flurried through the air with a slight wind. Would they be subjected to yet another great snowstorm?

He grimaced. He had no desire to forestall his departure for Grindleham indefinitely. It would be miserable and nostalgic in the worst ways to be confined to Norfield again due to the snow.

Alfred appeared at one of the windows lining the corridor at the base of the large staircase, a perplexed expression on his face. Upon hearing Hugh, he turned.

"What in heaven's name is Uncle Sid doing here again?" he said impatiently. "His bed is hardly cold, and we have had no time to replenish the stores of brandy and sherry he depleted a few days ago."

Alfred possibly liked Uncle Sid less than Uncle Sid liked him.

"I couldn't say for certain what brings him here again," Hugh said evasively, "but if this snow becomes heavier, we may well be looking at a protracted stay."

"Heaven help us!" Alfred said, appalled at the prospect.

Hugh only smiled, hoping that, by the end of his uncle's visit, Alfred would be singing a different tune.

In a matter of moments, Lord Siddington's boisterous voice carried from the entry hall to where they stood.

"Yes, and I'll take a glass of Dayton's best sherry in the drawing room," he said as he was being shown in.

Alfred sent a long-suffering glance at Hugh. They greeted their uncle, and Hugh led the way to the drawing room, knowing it would be useless to attempt any meaningful conversation with him until he had a drink in hand.

"Pleased to see you again, Uncle Sid," Alfred said without any evidence that he truly felt pleased, "and so soon after your last visit." He turned into the parlor doorway but stopped at the voice of his uncle.

"I think," Lord Siddington said, "that I have some news that might be of interest to you, Alfred. Join us in the drawing room, why don't you?"

Alfred looked as though he had grave doubts about his uncle being able to say anything of interest to him, but he was civil enough not to refuse such an invitation and nodded, following them down the corridor.

A quick-acting servant had clearly been before them to the drawing room, as a silver platter sat on the low table in front of the couches with a glass of brandy and the decanter next to it.

Hugh's patience began to wear as he watched his uncle inspect the brandy, smell it, and inquire of no one in particular of what origin the bottle was.

Alfred, though, was even more impatient. His mood had been sour ever since his meeting with Miss Bolton's father.

"Ah," Lord Siddington said, laying back on the couch with his arm resting on the end and closing his eyes. "Alfred, have you ever had a chance to visit Keldale?"

"No, I haven't had that pleasure." Alfred sent a significant look at Hugh as if to commiserate over the oddities of their uncle's conversation.

"Shame," said Lord Siddington. He paused, his eyes still closed. "How should you like to live there?"

Hugh attempted to suppress his smile, but without success. He thought he saw the vein in Alfred's forehead pulsate.

"I don't think I understand you, Uncle," Alfred said in a voice struggling to mask his annoyance and frustration.

"Lord Dunhaven has agreed to offer you the living at Keldale parish, as well as the one at Newmarsh."

Alfred's face went slack, and he blinked at his uncle, who opened his eyes and rearranged his position on the couch as though he had only asked Alfred his favorite brand of snuff.

"You would obviously employ a curate at Newmarsh," Lord Siddington said, "for I can tell you the parsonage at Keldale is the larger and better furnished of the two, besides being much closer to civilization. But between the livings, I think you and your *amour* might live comfortably."

Alfred stuttered. "I-I...but how...?"

"Do you think," Hugh said, unable to wait any longer, "that Miss Bolton's father will reconsider, knowing you have secured such a position?"

Alfred's jaw hung loose as he continued blinking, uncomprehending. "I think there may be a decent chance of it, yes." He turned toward Lord Siddington. "Why should Lord Dunhaven do such a thing for me? Or why should you, for that matter? You aren't even fond of me."

"Dash it, boy," Lord Siddington said, frowning, "what has fondness to say to any of it? We are family, are we not? Besides, it seems I am making a tradition out of gifting my nephews a living after their broken engagements."

Alfred rose from his seat and walked over to his uncle, putting out his arms in an invitation for an embrace. "Thank you, Uncle Sid," he said, his voice thick with emotion. "You can have no notion what this means to me."

Lord Siddington stared at him with a look of panic as his eyes moved from one outreached arm to the other. He recoiled a bit and said, "Save your embraces for Miss Bolton, I beg you."

Alfred dropped his arms and bowed. "As you please, Uncle. But please accept my most profound gratitude."

Lord Siddington waved a dismissive hand and drank from his glass.

Hugh sat back, taking a book from the table next to his chair, content to know that Alfred was rethinking his opinion of their uncle.

"I suppose," Alfred said, beginning to pace and rub his chin, "that I should write to Alice's father immediately, asking for another audience." He paused at the window, looking outside with a wistful expression.

"Be honest, Alfred," said Hugh with a half-smile. "You are considering throwing propriety out the window and asking that the carriage be brought around this very minute."

Alfred's brows snapped together, and his eyes narrowed as he continued peering through the window. "Who in the world...?"

Hugh frowned, closing his book and rising from his chair. "Another visitor? In this weather?"

Lord Siddington had his head back, oblivious to anything but his own comfort.

Hugh came up behind Alfred, squinting as he looked outside where the flurries seemed to have thickened and left a dusting of snow on the ground.

"Is that...?" Alfred said, leaning in closer to the window, and then rearing back a bit with a bemused look. "I believe that is the Caldwell's chaise."

Hugh stilled. Alfred was right. Pulling the carriage were the same two horses that had done so for a number of years. He swallowed, refusing to acknowledge the hope that had first jumped to his heart.

It must be Mr. Caldwell, of course—come to see Alfred himself, perhaps, though why he should have sent his engagement gift with Emma if he planned to come all along was anyone's guess.

The chaise came to a stop, and the postilion hopped down from the chestnut he had been riding, hastening to open the door.

Hugh's heart thumped as he watched a kid boot and the bottom of a green pelisse appear through the carriage door.

He froze.

Emma stepped carefully down to the ground, holding her bonnet to her head and squinting as her pelisse blew with the wind.

Hugh stifled a groan, torn between an overwhelming impatience and a dread of seeing Emma again. Perhaps he should have left that morning for Grindleham.

The postilion shut the chaise door behind Emma, leaving no room for wondering whether any other members of the Caldwell family had accompanied her. She was alone.

"Did Mama perhaps invite her?" Alfred asked, perplexed.

"I don't know. I shall go inquire of Mama myself."

Hugh strode from the room, grateful for a few moments to compose himself before having to face Emma. He rushed up the steps and down the corridor to the small sitting room his mother often spent the early afternoon in. He knocked gently, and it sounded faint compared to the pounding of his heart.

Hearing his mother's muted invitation to enter, he opened the door.

She was at her small escritoire, turned in her chair to see who had interrupted. She smiled upon seeing Hugh, gesturing for him to come in.

"I am sorry to disturb you, Mama," he said, stopping just past the threshold, "but I was wondering if you were expecting any visitors today?"

Her brows went up and she shook her head. "No, I wasn't. Is someone here? I thought I heard carriage wheels."

He chewed the inside of his lip. "Yes, Uncle Sid is here and has been for an hour or so. But Emma Caldwell has just arrived, I believe." He put his chin up, hoping that he sounded as nonchalant as his words.

His mother said nothing, but he could see the wheels turning in her head, and he could have sworn that he saw a smile tremble at the edge of her lips. But it was gone as quickly as it had appeared. "Hmm." She turned back to her writing, and Hugh stared, mystified by her response. Or lack of it.

"Do you not wish to see her, Mama?"

Her quill scratches continued. "I expect that it is not me she is here to see."

Receiving no indication that she intended to discuss things further, Hugh bemusedly stepped out of the room, closing the door softly behind him.

He paused a moment, taking in a deep breath.

Much as he wished he could let things take their course rather than discovering precisely what had brought Emma to Norfield on such a day, his patience would not allow it.

He rushed down the stairs and through the corridor, stopping at the drawing room door as he heard the sound of Emma's voice coming from within. His heart pounded, and he exhaled. He needed to regain control of himself.

The door opened in front of Hugh, revealing the back of Emma's head as she closed the door behind her. She looked up just in time to prevent a collision with Hugh.

He couldn't remember his heart beating so quickly or uncomfortably even in battle.

He bowed. " Miss Caldwell," he said.

She smiled at him in that particular way which couldn't but breed hope in his chest.

Grindleham. Tomorrow he would leave to Grindleham, no matter the weather. Anything but be subjected to that painfully alluring smile, knowing that it would be seen alongside Mr. Douglas for the rest of time.

"I was just coming in search of you," she said.

The words ought to have flattered him. But there was no hesitation in her manner, a fact which dampened his spirits even further. She seemed to be carrying on since their rift, unafflicted by any of the gloom and despair Hugh had been fighting for days.

"How may I be of service?" Hugh asked, hoping that whatever she required of him wouldn't necessitate lingering in her presence for any longer than was absolutely necessary. And yet hoping that it would.

"I was wondering," she said, lowering her eyes in a gesture of sudden shyness, "whether you would be agreeable to the terms I have set out for another truce."

A truce? Why in heaven's name would they need another truce?

He inclined his head civilly. "If you think another truce necessary, then I shall of course agree to whatever terms you see fit. I should perhaps inform you, though, that I will be absent from the district for the foreseeable future."

Her gaze flickered for a moment, and her face fell as she swallowed. "You are returning to your regiment?"

"No. I will be taking over my father's estate in Grindleham."

Her eyes widened. "In Derbyshire?"

He nodded, feeling an inkling of relief to see her dismay.

"That is a long way from here."

He grimaced. It was a very long way. A long way from those gray eyes and from those soft cheeks, still pink from the whipping wind outside.

Her mouth twisted to the side. "The truce will not work at such a distance, I am afraid."

He frowned. "What are the terms?"

She hesitated a moment, her eyes flicking upward to a place above him and then quickly back down, the corner of her mouth trembling slightly, fighting off a smile.

He followed the direction of her gaze, noticing the bough dangling above them. His gaze moved to her lips, and he forced them back up to her eyes.

"What?" he said, decisively dismissing the memory of the kiss they had shared by the light of the Christmas tree.

She offered no response, only keeping her gaze trained on him with twinkling eyes.

He frowned. "You mean not to tell me?"

Her mouth twisted to the side. "I have grossly overestimated your intellect, Lieutenant Warrilow. I was sure you would guess the terms."

He looked at her, baffled.

She tipped her head back, looking at the bough. "Will you do me a favor, Lieutenant?"

"What favor is that?" he said, suspicious of the funning humor she was in, unwilling to let himself overthink things.

"I believe there is one last berry on that bough"— she indicated it with her eyes. "It does not belong there."

He saw the spot of red, set against the verdant backdrop and looked at her with suspicion, plucking it off carefully.

She let out a laugh, the one he felt confident he would never tire of. "Perhaps it would be better to *show* you the gist of the truce," she said, looking up at him through her lashes and moving closer. She reached her arms up behind his neck and pulled him down toward her. Their lips barely touched, and he closed his eyes, his heart racing, hardly daring to believe what was happening.

"Do I need to explain more in depth?" she said, and he could feel her lips stretch outward in a smile.

"Perhaps so," he said, breathless.

"Gladly," she said, pressing her lips to his.

He needed no more encouragement than that, reaching for one of her hands which he clasped in his, wrapping it behind her and pulling her toward him for a kiss that was somehow even sweeter than the one they had shared a week ago.

She pulled away, and he let out a sigh of contentment or relief— perhaps both.

He stared into her eyes, noting the way her mouth still turned up at the side. His own mouth morphed into a responsive grin, but he shook his head bemusedly. "I don't understand. What changed?" he said.

"Nothing changed," she said. "I am simply possessed of the dearest, most selfless sister in the world who wishes for my happiness as much as her own." She raised a brow at him. "I don't pretend to understand what could possess you to desire me as a wife, but I am quite content that it be so."

"That you are so ignorant of your own charm and value is one thing I hope to cure you of. You are loyal and kind and"— he raised up his shoulders, searching for the words.

"Obstinate and misguided?" she offered.

He chuckled and toyed with one of her curls. "I have never met a woman who made me feel even a spark of what I've felt for you all these years, Emma. I don't deserve you or the happiness you bring me."

And he meant it. He didn't deserve it.

"That," she said, "is nonsense. I don't know how it comes to be that I am essential to your happiness, but I know that *you* are essential to mine. The past is behind us, whatever it has been, and the future—whatever it holds—we will face together."

He shut his eyes, breathing in the words. He cupped her cheek with his hand, and she leaned into it, closing her eyes and cradling his hand with hers.

He leaned in for another slow, soft kiss and then pulled away, looking up at the bough above. "We need more berries."

She threw her head back and laughed that delightful sound he would hear for the rest of his life.

EPILOGUE

The lights on the Christmas tree twinkled in the corner of the drawing room, and two small children watched nearby, their eyes alight with fascination.

"Not too close, Francine," said Emma, untangling her arm from her husband's, standing up, and walking toward the tree.

Two of the lights flickered and went out with a puff of air, and the children giggled as Emma picked up Francine in one arm with an indulgent smile and grasped the hand of her nephew Johnathan with her free hand.

She handed Johnathan off to her brother-in-law George, who set him down firmly between himself and Lucy on the couch.

"Blow it out!" said Francine with a pout. "I want to blow it out!"

"How many candles is that tonight?" Hugh said, stretching his arm out to welcome Emma and Francine back to the couch and taking his squirming daughter in his arms.

"Six," said Emma, sitting snugly next to him and smoothing out her skirts.

Lieutenant Warrilow held Francine in front of him on his knees, narrowing his eyes as he looked at her in mock anger. "And many more if you were capable of blowing properly." He blew in Francine's face, and she squeezed her eyes shut before giggling.

"How is Mrs. Seymour, Hugh?" Emma asked.

He bounced Francine on his knee, smiling at her. "Very well, I believe. She has remarried, you know—a man who acts as butler for the Talbots."

Emma hadn't known, but she was relieved to hear it. Mrs. Seymour and her children had been a source of frequent conversation and concern for Hugh over the past few years.

The door opened, and Alfred appeared, holding it open for his wife who had one hand below her round belly and one on her back.

"Alice!" said Emma in surprise.

Hugh hurried to set down Francine, getting up simultaneously with George as they rushed to assist Alice Warrilow to a seat.

"We weren't expecting you," said Lucy, letting her son wriggle off her lap, "but how happy we are to see you!"

"Yes," said Alice between labored breaths as she was lowered into her seat with the help of all three men. "We had not intended to come, but I told Alfred that I could even bear a bumpy carriage ride so long as it meant spending a few hours away from the parsonage."

"It is terrible being confined and so restless, isn't it?" Emma said with a sympathetic smile. "You are very near the end, so take comfort." Emma paused a moment and looked a question at Hugh, who inclined his head with a half-smile. "And I," she said on a breath, "am at the beginning all over again."

Heads whipped around, and an intake of breath was heard from both Alice and Lucy, both of them exclaiming at the news.

"How wonderful," Lucy said, stooping down to embrace Emma. "I shall pray that this baby has a strong disposition to equal Francine's."

Emma feigned offense, but Hugh laughed. "She does take after you, doesn't she, Emma? Stubborn"— he pushed himself up from the couch, rushing over to Francine who had walked noiselessly to the

Christmas tree again, sending a mischievous look over her shoulder —"little lady."

Alice grimaced and put a hand to her belly.

"Perhaps," said George, watching her with a frown, "we should fetch the doctor as a precaution."

Alfred was regarding his wife with a brow knit tightly. He shook his head. "I should not have let you convince me to come, my love," he said, moving to pull the bell.

Alice raised up a hand and shook her head. "No, no, please. I don't need a doctor."

Alfred looked ready to do battle over the issue, and Alice sighed before saying, "I promise I shall tell you if anything changes. The last thing I wish to do is disturb Doctor Brady on Christmas evening."

Her husband hesitated with his hand on the bell but then dropped it to his side. "As you wish." He walked over and stooped down to kiss her atop the head.

A sudden scuffle broke out, and all heads turned toward Francine and Johnathan, whose arms were interlocked in a battle for one of the paper flowers adorning the tree.

"Oh dear," said Emma. She and Lucy both raced over to extricate their children.

"I despise you, Johnny!" said Francine, swiping at him and then making one last grab for the flower.

Emma shot a significant look at her husband and then suppressed a smile at Lucy who was trying not to laugh.

"What?" Emma said.

Lucy gripped her lips together and shrugged innocently. "She is very much like you. That is all."

Emma scoffed. "I insist that you take that back."

Lucy looked at her, incredulous. "Only a few years ago, you were treating Hugh very much the same way as Francine is treating Johnathan."

Emma's mouth twisted to the side, acknowledging the hit.

"Johnny is rude, Papa," Francine said to Hugh, as if on cue. "I don't like playing with him!"

"Oh, come, Francie," he said, shooting a quick, impish glance at his wife. "Have a little goodwill for the gentleman."

Francine scowled.

Emma and Hugh walked over to their daughter, Emma stooping down so that she was at eye-level with Francine. "Perhaps, my dear, you might consider a truce with Johnny?" She leaned in closer, whispering loudly, "If you only *pretend* to like him, you may just find that he is not *quite* so terrible as you think him."

Hugh and Emma met eyes, hers twinkling at him.

"Stirring praise, my dear," he said softly through his half-smile, leaning in to kiss her.

PREVIEW OF THE EARL'S MISTLETOE MATCH

BY ASHTYN NEWBOLD

CHAPTER ONE

Andrew Dawson, the Earl of Whitfield, stood on the outskirts of the ballroom, surveying the crowd of unrecognizable people. The masquerade theme was intriguing, with credit to his host, Lord Trenton, but quite unfortunate when one was in search of a particular lady.

Andrew adjusted his mask at the corners, ensuring it was symmetrical. He traced his gaze over every young lady in the room. Esther Lockwood was a beauty, so she should not have been so difficult to find, but the difficulty was in the many masks—and his very short acquaintance with the girl. They had only been introduced two weeks before, and she had been quite soft-spoken and timid. He had not had enough time to glimpse the intricacies of her character, nor get any idea of what her favorite animal might have been.

That information would have been extremely useful at the moment.

A fox, a peacock, and a doe walked past as Andrew stared into the crowd, but none of the masquerading women had the same hair as Esther, at least not visible from behind their dominos. Long and honey-blonde.

Blast the masks.

As soon as he found her, he could ask her to dance. His father was growing quite impatient to hear of his progress on the courtship he was supposed to have established weeks ago. He would not have been bothered to attend the masquerade that evening if he had not suspected Esther would be in attendance. Miss Lockwood was beautiful, well-mannered, neat, and came with a sizeable dowry. There was little else Andrew could hope for in a marriage. Things such as love and affection...he had long since abandoned hope of.

But he was beginning to abandon hope of courting Miss Lockwood at all. She had been nothing but elusive and distant. She seemed to care little for furthering their acquaintance, something Andrew was not accustomed to in the slightest.

As he considered his next tactic for catching Esther's attention, a large hand clapped over his shoulder. He jerked around in surprise.

"Whitfield, I thought you despised Christmas festivities." Martin Fusgrove, a flirt almost as notorious as himself, stood behind Andrew in a broad lion mask. Andrew would not have recognized him if not for his jovial voice and familiarity. There were few people Andrew would call his friends, but Fusgrove was one of them. Fur lined the outskirts of Fusgrove's head and mask, intricate golden details forming the features of a lion. "Where is your costume?" His friend's eyes widened behind his mask, as if appalled by Andrew's lack of conformity.

Did Fusgrove know him at all?

Andrew crossed his arms, fully aware of the boring nature of his plain black venetian mask in comparison to the extravagant appearances of the many gentlemen in attendance. Andrew did not have to dress so horrendously to catch attention. It was one of the many advantages of being an earl. "I do despise Christmas festivities," he said with a sigh. "I am only here because my father is eager to hear of the progress of my nonexistent courtship with Miss Lockwood when I travel home next week."

Fusgrove chuckled. "Have you even spoken to her?"

Andrew could think of two sentences he had exchanged with Miss Lockwood, but neither were memorable enough for him to remember the content. "Yes," he stammered. "We have spoken. But if I am to provide my parents with the desired answers to their inquiries about Miss Lockwood without lying, I ought to find her this evening." Andrew drew a heavy breath, only now realizing just how anxious he sounded. He rubbed his hands against his trousers, avoiding his friend's intent gaze. "I have chosen to wear a simple mask so Miss Lockwood will recognize me, should I approach her. The problem I am now facing, however, is that Miss Lockwood did not give me the same courtesy."

Andrew's gaze swept over the crowd once again, finding a great variety of costumes and masked ladies, but none that he could confidently determine to be Esther. Perhaps if she hadn't avoided him at the last party, then he could have been more familiar with her voice and smile. Had he ever seen her smile? He couldn't quite recall the image. What color were her eyes? Blue? Brown? He hadn't the slightest idea. It had not struck him until now that he should have payed greater attention to her at the Townshend's soiree.

Fusgrove laughed under his breath, sending a surge of annoyance through Andrew's chest. There was nothing humorous about his situation. He despised courting. If he could have it his way, he would remain single for all of his days. The only woman he had ever loved, Abigail, had broken his heart, and he had no intention of letting it be broken again. No—he would not even take the risk. One did not trust a fine dish in the hands of a careless child. It was to be locked up in the cupboard, out of reach and out of sight. Andrew had done the same with his heart for the last year, and he had finally achieved some sense of repair, of peace. Now he simply had to secure a wife that would appease his father's demands and be done with it.

There were a great number of women he could have chosen from, but Miss Lockwood had always been his mother's favorite. Thus, his father's. She was wealthy and came from a highly esteemed family. If his efforts tonight resulted in another failure...his stomach twisted at the thought of disappointing his parents again. They had chosen Abigail for him, and he had failed. What would they think if he failed all over again?

When Andrew remembered that Fusgrove still watched him, he squared his shoulders, hiding any trace of insecurity and worry.

Fusgrove scratched at his chin, the only part of his face that was not covered. The mask lifted on his cheeks as he smiled. "There is one thing you might do to... shall we say... bolster your progress."

Andrew eyed his friend's smile, which was fully ripe with mischief. It took only three seconds for Andrew to catch his meaning. "No. We agreed last December that the tradition was to be abandoned."

Fusgrove swatted his hand through the air. "Nonsense. I recall no such conversation."

"Well, I do."

"I do not trust your memory at the moment, as you cannot even recall enough about Miss Lockwood to locate her in this ballroom."

Andrew heaved a sigh, rubbing his left temple. A headache was coming on.

"I carried out the tradition last year," Fusgrove said. "I believe it is now your turn. I can think of no better time nor place for you to do it." He leaned closer. "I believe I caught sight of a lovely bundle of mistletoe hanging above the archway near the servant's quarters."

Andrew couldn't stop his smile of disbelief. "Are you suggesting that I locate Miss Lockwood, by some miracle, and guide her away from all spectators to the mistletoe in order to steal a kiss that is likely to frighten her out of her wits? I do not think that will help my situation."

Fusgrove chuckled. "*I* would certainly consider a kiss from you to be quite frightening, but a young girl such as she may find it pleasant.

You are one of the most sought after bachelors in this ballroom, after all."

As if to affirm his claim, a group of young ladies walked past, all eyes fixed on Andrew behind their masks. Giggles and whispers floated up, mingling with the lively music.

"Your insecurity baffles me," Fusgrove said. "With a bit of luck, the young lady will be smitten out of her wits and you may marry her before twelfth night. Your parents will be pleased with your achievement and you may return to enjoying parties instead of being anxious the entire time."

In truth, Andrew hadn't enjoyed parties for the last year. If not for the prodding of his parents, he would have simply stayed locked up in his London home and avoided social events altogether. He refrained from offering a grumbled contradiction, and instead regarded his friend with skepticism. "*If* I intend to carry on the tradition, how do you plan to locate Miss Lockwood? I am not even certain she is here."

Fusgrove joined Andrew in scanning the room, facing the crowd from their place near the wall. "I see the majority of the women are brunettes, but I also see several have their hair hidden behind their dominos."

"Precisely. Do you now understand my difficulty?"

"Indeed." Fusgrove drummed his fingers against his opposite arm before letting out a soft gasp. "There. Do you see the two women standing side by side in the corner?"

Andrew followed his gaze to the far corner of the ballroom, where two women stood, of equal height and size. Both women had long, curled hair, pulled up to the crown of their heads. Neither wore a domino to cover it, but both wore masks. One woman appeared to be dressed in a rabbit costume, two tall ears extending up from her bejeweled mask, and a fur wrapped about her shoulders. The other woman wore a simple white mask and silver gown, standing even further into the shadows than her companion.

One of them must have been Esther, and if Andrew were to

venture a guess, he would say she was the woman in the simple white mask. Only one as timid as Esther would choose not to stand out at an event like this. But even as plain as the mask was, it hid most of her face, leaving just her eyes and lips visible, but none of her bone structure and eyebrows, which he was beginning to realize gave away much of a person's identity. From what he could see of the two ladies, they could very well have been the same person.

"Do you think we have found her?" Fusgrove asked in a quiet voice. "I have not been introduced to Miss Lockwood. Does she have a sister?"

As Andrew stared at the two women, he began to wonder the same thing. His mother had given him a detailed description of Miss Lockwood's family, and she had only mentioned a brother.

"I don't believe so."

"Then who is the other lady? Which lady is Miss Lockwood?"

"I don't know." Andrew chewed the inside of his cheek in frustration. "I have told you before, I am not well-acquainted with her. We have only spoken at close proximity once during our introduction two weeks ago. She avoided my gaze and hardly spoke a word."

"I see." Fusgrove's fingers drummed faster. "I suppose you must choose which lady is more likely to be Miss Lockwood and approach her. At an event such as this, you must be willing to risk being wrong. The worst outcome would be her kindly correcting you and redirecting your attention to the true Miss Lockwood."

Andrew's heart rose to his throat with anxiety. He would be the first to admit he put on airs. Airs of security, confidence, and, at times, arrogance. How else could he hide the things he truly felt? Vulnerability was equal to weakness in his opinion, and if there was anything he refused to be it was *weak*. He put on a smile, one he employed often in public—broad and charming—some had even called it devilish.

"Very well." Andrew grabbed Fusgrove by the arm. "You are coming with me."

"What do you plan to do?"

"I am going to ask her to dance, and, if an opportunity arises, we will slip away to find that mistletoe you spoke of." Andrew willed his confidence to grow, but he only felt more nervous.

Fusgrove laughed. "That is the Whitfield I know. Welcome back." He dropped a bow. "I have missed you."

Andrew straightened his mask again, catching the eye of the lady in the white mask. Was it really Miss Esther Lockwood? He turned to his friend. "If I am to carry out the tradition, then you'll have to distract the other lady."

Fusgrove shook his arm free of Andrew's grasp and followed willingly, putting on a smile of his own. "Fortunately for you, I am quite skilled at distracting ladies."

Continue reading The Earl's Mistletoe Match on Amazon or Kindle Unlimited

ALSO IN THIS SERIES

OTHER TITLES BY MARTHA KEYES

If you enjoyed this book, make sure to check out my other books:

Families of Dorset Series:

Wyndcross: A Regency Romance (Book One)

Isabel: A Regency Romance (Book Two)

Cecilia: A Regency Romance (Book Three)

Hazelhurst: A Regency Romance (Book Four)

Phoebe: A Regency Romance (Series Novelette)

Other Titles:

Eleanor: A Regency Romance

ACKNOWLEDGMENTS

Thank you first and foremost to my wonderful fellow authors in the Belles of Christmas series. Mindy, Ashtyn, Deborah, and Kasey have all become good friends and authors for whom I hold a great deal of respect.

My mom, Karen Maxwell, as always, has been a cheerleader and editor from the beginning.

My husband has again given up precious works hours of his own in order for me to write, edit, write, edit, *ad nauseum*. My little boys are almost always good sports about their scatterbrained mom and my constant sneaking away to the computer to get down an idea while it's fresh.

Thank you to my editor, Jenny Proctor, for her wonderful feedback—I'm so glad I have you!

Thank you to my Review Team for your help and support in an often nerve-wracking business.

And thank you to all my fellow Regency authors and to the wonderful communities of The Writing Gals and LDS Beta Readers. I would be lost without all of your help and trailblazing!

ABOUT THE AUTHOR

Martha Keyes was born, raised, and educated in Utah—a home she loves dearly but also dearly loves to escape, whenever she can travel the world. She received a BA in French Studies and a Master of Public Health, both from Brigham Young University.

Word crafting has always fascinated and motivated her, but it wasn't until a few years ago that she considered writing her own stories. When she isn't writing, she is honing her photography skills, looking for travel deals, and spending time with her husband and children. She lives with her husband and twin boys in Vineyard, Utah.

Made in the USA
Monee, IL
01 January 2020